MISSING
Three Days in Jerusalem

Sonia Falaschi-Ray

Matador
9 Priory Business Park,
Wistow Road, Kibworth Beauchamp,
Leicestershire. LE8 0RX
Tel: (+44) 116 279 2299
Fax: (+44) 116 279 2277
Email: books@troubador.co.uk
Web: www.troubador.co.uk/matador

ISBN 978 1783060 429

British Library Cataloguing in Publication Data.
A catalogue record for this book is available from the British Library.

Typeset by Troubador Publishing Ltd, Leicester, UK

Matador is an imprint of Troubador Publishing Ltd

Printed and bound in the UK by TJ International, Padstow, Cornwall

The Word became flesh and dwelt among us.
Any resemblance to any persons alive or dead is
entirely intentional.

Dedication

To my husband, John, whose extensive knowledge of the ancient world has been invaluable, to my mother Enid for her unswerving support and to our golden retrievers, Quintus and Rufus, on whose walks much of this book was composed.

TABLE OF CONTENTS

TABLE OF CONTENTS

ACKNOWLEDGEMENTS

My thanks to these people who have all helped in editing, design, furnishing ideas and encouragement: Enid Falaschi, Mirjam Foot, Malcolm Guite, Annie Gurner, Kieran Hood, John Ingoldby, Elizabeth Mackay, William Mackay, Billie Palmer, John Ray, Christina Rees and Mike Thompson.

PRINCIPAL PROTAGONISTS IN ORDER OF APPEARANCE

Joseph Bar-Janni (of Arimathea): A Member of the Jewish ruling council in whose tomb Jesus was buried. In this story he is a rich merchant and a second cousin of Jesus' mother, Miriam (Mary); he has a wife, Ruth*, sons, Heli*, Janni* and a daughter Rachel*.

Shabaka*: A Nubian nobleman, and a former slave in Egypt who enters Joseph of Arimathea's household.

Miriam: (Mary) mother of Yeshua (Jesus) and wife of Jo (Joseph). In this story she has younger children: James, who becomes leader of the church in Jerusalem, and Sarah*.

Jo: (Joseph), husband of Miriam and adoptive father of Yeshua (Jesus).

Yeshua Bar Joseph: (Jesus) son of Miriam, (Mary), and of God, conceived by the Holy Spirit. He is the Messiah, the Christ, the Saviour of the world. Adopted son of Jo.

Nicodemus: Rabbi who visits the adult Jesus in secret to learn about his message and who is present at his burial.

John: John the Baptist, son of the priest Zechariah and his wife Elizabeth, who is an elderly cousin of Miriam (Mary).

Simon of Cyrene: Singled out from the crowd to carry Jesus' cross after he had collapsed. He had sons called Alexander and Rufus.

Caiaphas: High Priest who instigated Jesus' arrest and crucifixion.

Eleazar★: husband of Judith★, parents of Martha and Mary-Beth (Mary) and Lazarus, who live in Bethany, a village just to the east of Jerusalem.

Martha: Friend of Yeshua, (Jesus), sister of Mary–Beth, (Mary) and Lazarus, living in Bethany.

Mary-Beth: see above.

Judas: One of Jesus' twelve disciples, who betrayed him to the Temple authorities.

Peter: One of Jesus' disciples. Originally called Simon Bar-Jonah.

Philetus: The 'beloved' disciple in John's Gospel. Probably the evangelist, John himself.

Lazarus: Brother of Martha and Mary-Beth, whom Jesus had raised from the dead.

Magda: (Mary Magdalene), a disciple of Jesus of whom it is written that she had seven demons cast out of her.

John-Mark: Companion of St Paul later in the New Testament. Thought to be the author of Mark's Gospel, an amanuensis of Peter. Tradition suggests that the Last Supper was held in his family's house.

Pontius Pilate: Roman Prefect of Judea, Procurator and Governor of Palestine AD 26-36.

★ Imaginary persons who do not appear in the Gospel record.

PROLOGUE

OFF THE COAST OF ALEXANDRIA, EGYPT c. 15 BC

The end is in the beginning

Crash! *Leviathan* lurched onto her starboard side and failed to right herself as waves creamed over the deck, poured into the cockpit and soaked the crew. Two sailors wrestled with the tiller. A third, Ishmael, was almost washed into the sea. Crack! The storm-sail split in the wind. The ship became unsteerable, her mast dipping low. She was being forced by the wind and waves onto a lee shore.

'Throw everything you can overboard!' ordered the captain.

But it was too late. Most of the cargo was Egyptian granite. It was that which had snapped its lashings and shifted in the hold, causing the ship to list.

'This is all your doing! You know that, Master Joseph. I should never have listened to you, allowing you to override my judgement!' shouted the captain.

His words were whipped away by the wind, but Joseph knew what he was saying. They could barely keep their footing on the water-washed deck. With each wave the ship listed more steeply.

'We should throw *him* overboard!' snarled Ishmael. 'It's all his fault. If he wasn't in such a hurry, we'd be safe in Alex.'

Suddenly *Leviathan* juddered as her stern ran aground, sticking fast in sand. The rudder twisted, hurling the helmsmen against the cockpit's edge, snapping various ribs and mangling an arm.

'I'll go overboard!' shouted Joseph. 'Maybe the Lord will have mercy on you once I'm gone.' He unsheathed his knife to cut his tether, but fumbled in the wet.

'Look! Another vessel!' shouted Ishmael. 'It's an Egyptian galley.'

Indeed it was, appearing through the spray. With her shallower draft she could venture further towards the shore and her oars, combined with sails, made her more manoeuvrable than *Leviathan*. The galley positioned herself downwind of them, using her port-side oars to hold position and shipping some of her starboard ones. Her crew threw a scrambling net from the deck, trailing it into the sea. The galley's helmsman struggled to keep her steady, as her crew gestured to the men on the stricken vessel to jump and swim. Most of them couldn't swim, but fear furnished the skill. The captain cut the ropes holding the injured helmsmen. Timing his jump, he grabbed the more disabled man and struck out for the net. He reached it with one hand, but got knocked back by the swell. Coughing and struggling, and with an almost superhuman effort, he got the man onto the net. Sailors hauled him aboard. The captain returned for the other injured man. Joseph cut the remaining sailors' tethering lines and almost bodily threw them overboard. He counted, seven, eight … Where were the other two? Perhaps they were below and couldn't get the hatch open, now it was submerged. He plunged forward through the chest-high water, felt down for the hatch and wrenched it open. The sea poured in but the men's heads appeared.

The first out stared at Joseph angrily. Despite the danger, he was determined to have his say. 'You'll kill us all you stupid, ignorant, arrogant boy! How dare you pull rank on the skipper? I've sailed all over with him and he's always kept his crew safe. The first time you're here without your father you insist on sailing out into a storm just to get to Joppa first. *Impress Papa, get the best prices.* Well he won't be impressed now will he?'

A wave soaked them but he hadn't finished.

'This was going to be my last trip. I've a bit put by. My second grandchild's on the way. We've got a smallholding in the Judean hills. We'd have managed. Your arrogance could have made widows of all our wives.'

'I'm sorry.'

'No use in saying sorry. You can't make it better, can you? You can't master the sea, you don't rule the waves.'

The ship groaned as it settled into the sand, then shuddered as its back started to break. Joseph helped the two men across the deck and they flung themselves into the boiling foam between the ships. He saw them reach the net and be helped aboard. He clung to the half-submerged deck-rail. The buffeting, wet and cold had exhausted him. He was aware of the galley crew's frantic gesturing. Should he go down with the ship? An image of his mother entered his mind. She would be distraught if he drowned. She had been so anxious about him going alone for the first time. His father had reassured her that the captain had never lost a ship, nor lost a man to an avoidable accident; a remarkable feat. Now he, Joseph, had thrown away not just a valuable cargo of granite but *Leviathan*, pride of his father's fleet. He thought the men were safe. In despair he prayed aloud, 'Please Lord, don't let my pride cause any of these men to be drowned. Find them a safe harbour. May no blame attach to the captain. Forgive my pride. If I can ever make amends please spare my life to allow me to do so. I'll always thank you and I'll pay what I've promised. Deliverance belongs to the Lord!'

A wave picked him up and flung him off the deck. He thrashed in the water, attempting to reach the galley. His sodden clothes weighed him down and the swell sucked him away. He sank. It was over.

A hand grabbed his chin from behind, lifting his head clear. Joseph gasped for breath. He couldn't see who held him, but he was a strong swimmer. Making headway, his rescuer grabbed the net and bodily boosted Joseph up it, into the arms of the crew. He collapsed exhausted onto the deck of the galley. Vaguely he heard shouted orders and the vessel got under way, running before the wind, heading for the port of Alexandria. *Leviathan*'s deck was barely visible above the waves. The lookout strained to catch a first glimpse of the beam from the world-famous lighthouse, which would guide them safely home.

Later, Joseph sat up and saw his rescuer squatting on his haunches gazing at him. He was a huge, muscular Nubian, some twenty years of age. He had an amulet around his neck of the Nubian god Apedemak, a man with a lion's head. He wore an oiled leather jacket, trousers and boots.

'You saved my life. How can I thank you? My name is Joseph Bar-Janni. My father owned that ship.'

'I am Shabaka. I was once a nobleman in my own land but now I am a slave of this galley's owner.'

'I will buy your freedom for you, if it costs my entire inheritance. Then you may then stay with us or we will pay your passage back to your home.'

PART 1
JUDEA c. AD 5

CHAPTER 1

Caravanserai

Matti's inn appeared as they rounded a bend in the road. It was a welcome sight after a long slog north through the Judean hills. Six families, all from the same town, had journeyed together along with their baggage animals. This was their first evening of a five-day journey, travelling home from Jerusalem. Jo, Miriam and their young children, James and Sarah, plus their donkey, Rosie, arrived in a group. It had been a dusty trek and the assorted children ensured slow progress. The inn's terracotta walls rose in front of them, and a large courtyard was just visible through an archway.

'We're finally here!' exclaimed Miriam. 'I'm exhausted. Jo, could you get us that room we had on the way down? I tried to reserve it, but Matti wouldn't promise.'

'All right Miriam, I'll just see to Rosie,' Jo replied.

Miriam glared at him. 'Oh, leave the donkey till you get the room!'

Jo grimaced and shrugged. Handing the halter rope to his nephew, Ben, he said, 'Please see she has water and food, I'll be along in a minute. By the way, have you seen Yeshua?'

'No. Why?'

'We haven't seen him, and I thought he was travelling with you boys.'

'Sorry. I haven't seen him all day, but he must be here somewhere.'

The courtyard of the inn was busy with people, along with numerous donkeys and the odd scavenging dog. Jo made his

3

way towards a red-faced, burly man shouting orders and greeting guests.

'Good evening Master Joseph! Yes, yes I know your good lady wants the Lily Room. It's ready for you now. The boy will take your things. Samuel! Take Master Joseph's pack up to the Lily Room.'

Matti turned away, hot and sweaty, tripped over a small dog and swore under his breath. He was immediately caught by a mother with a crying baby who needed to clean him up. Now!

Miriam, taking eight-year-old James and Sarah, six, by the hand, joined Ben with some neighbourhood boys, who were congregated around a food stall. The smell was delicious, roasting meat mingled with wood smoke, masking less attractive odours.

'Hello Ben.'

'Good evening Auntie Miriam.'

'Are you sure you haven't seen Yeshua?'

'No, I really can't say I have.'

'Wasn't he travelling with you?'

'No, but he might have been with Matt and Josh, I think I saw them going up there.' He gestured to a first-floor door at the top of some outside stairs.

'Thank you Ben. James, please stay with Ben and look after Sarah.'

'But Mama, she's *so* boring.'

'James, don't talk like that about your sister! And don't wander off.'

A faint frown of worry creased Miriam's forehead. She brushed the thought aside. It was just like Yesh to go off on his own with no thought of unpacking Rosie. He used to be such a helpful little lad, but recently he had gone all dreamy and distant. I suppose it's just his age, she thought, and he has been studying hard for his bar mitzvah.

She climbed the stairs. The flaking lime-wash was still warm from the heat of the day. She glanced through the opening to where Jo's brother Daniel, and his wife Hannah, were unpacking. Matt and Josh were fencing with newly acquired wooden swords.

'Careful or you'll have someone's eye out!' came Hannah's voice.

Miriam tapped tentatively on the door. 'Can I come in?'

'Oh, hi Miriam, come on in and sit down,' said Hannah.

'No, I won't stay. Have you seen Yeshua?'

'No, I haven't seen him all day. Boys, have you seen him?'

'Who?'

'Yeshua. Miriam was just asking.'

'No,' said Matt. 'Me neither,' said Josh. They resumed fencing.

'Oh well, I'm sure he's around somewhere.' Miriam turned and scanned the courtyard, a large dusty space surrounded by four mud-brick walls with terracotta patches showing though the lime-wash. It was still packed with people and luggage, although most of the donkeys had been stabled. A large wooden door was set in the centre of the south side, next to which was a porter's lodge. The door would be bolted at sunset. The eastern block contained a spacious room where guests could congregate and eat. At one end was a huge bread oven and roasting spit, as well as an iron stove on which cooking pots steamed, emitting a fragrance of onions and herbs. The stables took up much of the western block, along with storerooms. The northern block and most of the first floor contained guestrooms. The innkeeper, Matti, and his family lived above the gate. Stairs ran up to the flat roof on which tents were erected during the summer, when it was cooler to sleep in the open. Most of the windows opened into the courtyard with only a few positioned in the outside walls. This enabled the building to be enclosed like a fortress, which had been necessary during more turbulent times. In the centre of the courtyard was a covered well, with a bucket and pulley system for ease of use. A bitch and her puppies were lying in its shade and a small girl was playing with them. Over in one corner stood a lemon tree, surrounded by a low wall.

Miriam strained for a sight of her eldest son. He would soon be deemed a man, although in many ways he was still her little boy. Nothing. She couldn't see him anywhere. No matter, he might well be up in one of his friends' rooms and would be bound to turn up for supper. However, a knot of fear had formed in her stomach and she couldn't shake off her anxiety.

As the sun dipped over the western hills the men congregated for evening prayers. Facing south, towards Jerusalem, they placed their prayer shawls over their heads, held up their hands and, led by their rabbi, started to recite the familiar words.

'Hear O Israel, the Lord our God, the Lord is One. Blessed be the name of his glorious kingdom for ever and ever. And you shall love the Lord your God with all your heart and with all your soul and with all your might. And these words that I command you today shall be in your heart. And you shall teach them diligently to your children, and you shall speak of them …'

Miriam tuned out of the rhythmic chanting and scanned the courtyard again. The cicadas were just starting their nightly din, almost in competition with the men. Perhaps they were also acknowledging their Maker? Miriam remained on the stairs until the prayer drew to its end.

'I am the Lord, your God, who led you from the land of Egypt to be a God to you. I am the Lord, your God. Amen.'

She hurried down and headed for the Lily Room, just as Jo

emerged. 'I can't find Yesh anywhere,' she said, her voice rising with anxiety.

'Well he must be somewhere, let's look for him systematically,' he replied.

'I've been up to Daniel's and Ben hasn't seen him all day and …'

'Darling, calm down. I'm sure it'll be all right. He is twelve after all; he's not a child any more.'

'But anything could have happened to him if he's not here! Why couldn't you keep an eye on him? Why do I always have to do everything? Did he say anything to you?'

'Well he mentioned he just had to see someone before we left, but I told him not to be long.'

'You what!' she shouted. 'You let him go off just as we were leaving? How could you? He could be anywhere.'

'Now we can't be certain he's not with us and I'm sure he's fine,' Jo replied. 'Look, I'll take the west and north blocks, you try the south and east and we'll meet in the dining room. All right?'

She nodded and hurried off.

★★★

Later that evening they had a family conference. Yeshua clearly wasn't with them. Miriam was all for going straight back to Jerusalem, even though there was only a half moon and the roads, safe enough during the day, were not incident-free at night, even with armed guards; and that was supposing you could see where you were going. Jo promised they would set off at first light, leaving Hannah to take care of James and Sarah, as the rest of the party continued north. He tried to reassure Miriam.

'Daniel is lending us a donkey so we can travel back faster.'

7

'Not Thistle. Rosie doesn't like Thistle. She gets on with Saffron.'

'Of course you can have Saffron,' said Daniel.

Miriam nervously ate another honey cake. She had never understood how people went off their food when they were worried. It always made her ravenous. Yeshua would be hungry. Did he have any money on him? Where would he sleep? You heard of boys being abducted. On and on her thoughts whirled.

Later that evening, when they were all in bed, Miriam stared up at the ceiling, terrified at what might have become of Yesh. Jo's calmness was comforting in some ways but also maddening. Wasn't he worried?

'Of course I'm worried,' he said quietly, reading her thoughts. 'However, you should try and get some sleep now and we'll set off as soon as it's light. I promise.'

She shivered. It was still chilly at night even though they were tucked up under rough linen sheets and two thick woollen blankets of mottled brown, fawn and cream. The moonlight filtered through a crack in the shutters. She listened to the regular breathing of her other two children. The time crawled by. Never before had she looked forward so much to the cock's first crow. She tried to pray. Psalm 121 came to her:

I will lift up mine eyes unto the hills, from whence cometh my help?
My help cometh from the Lord, which made heaven and earth.
He will not suffer thy foot to be moved: he that keepeth thee will not slumber.
Behold, he that keepeth Israel shall neither slumber nor sleep.
The Lord is thy keeper: the Lord is thy shade upon thy right hand.
The sun shall not smite thee by day, nor the moon by night.
The Lord shall preserve thee from all evil: he shall preserve thy soul.
The Lord shall preserve thy going out and thy coming in from this time forth, and even for evermore.

She slept fitfully, dreaming of seeing Yeshua disappearing through a far gateway. She tried to shout but no sound came. Searching, searching, always frustrated.

Jerusalem in the time of Jesus

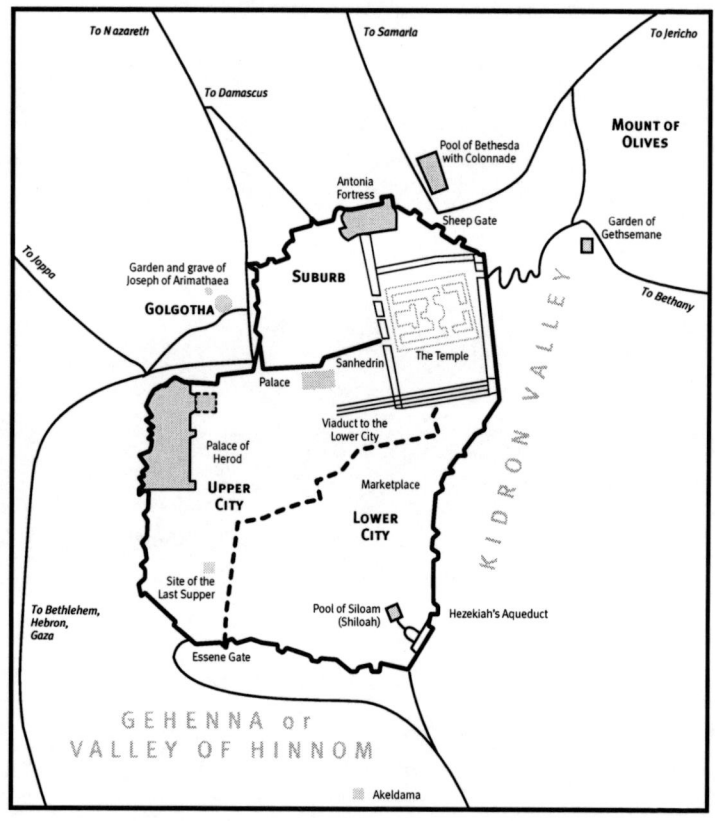

CHAPTER 2

A close-run thing

It was the hour before sunset. The shadow cast by the high walls put the Temple courtyard into shade; just a single shaft of light came through the open gateway. The courtyard was emptying, with stallholders packing up and the cleaners starting to sweep away the debris of the day. Not many came to sacrifice at the Temple just after Passover, so there had been fewer animals in than usual, easing their task.

Yeshua realised with some alarm that his parents must be long gone. He had just nipped back to the Temple as they were preparing to leave. It always took ages to get everyone organised so he was sure he'd be fine. He'd encountered two rabbis debating about whether there was life after death or whether, once you went down to Sheol, that was it, oblivion. He found it fascinating seeing how each used the authority of scripture to bolster his own case. One was a Pharisee, an expert in the Law, who was convinced that there was an afterlife, and that the coming Messiah would herald in a new kingdom on earth, mirroring the one ruled by the Almighty. The other, a Sadducee, a member of the Jewish upper class, disagreed.

The Pharisee opined, 'There is much scriptural evidence that the soul lives on after death. What about the prophet Elijah being taken up bodily into Heaven? Or when King Saul was bereft because the Spirit of the Lord had abandoned him and he wanted to know why. He disguised himself and consulted the Witch of Endor to raise the spirit of the prophet Samuel, who appeared. If there was no afterlife for anyone, that couldn't have happened. Perhaps it is just for us, the Lord's chosen people? And only the righteous ones at that.'

The Sadducee responded, 'There is nothing after death. Sheol is just a term, a name for the pit, oblivion. We know what happens to the body, it disintegrates. The soul cannot exist without a body, it just disappears.'

'What about justice?' asked the Pharisee. 'Given that the wicked often flourish until their death, retaining wealth and power until their end. How is the Lord to administer justice if there is no afterlife in which to do so?'

'Justice isn't applicable to only one individual,' the Sadducee replied. 'The Lord's justice may be demonstrated by the fortunes of a man's descendants. Remember when the Lord appeared to Moses in the cloud and proclaimed:

'The Lord God, merciful and gracious, longsuffering, and abundant in goodness and truth. Keeping mercy for thousands, forgiving iniquity and transgression and sin, and that will by no means clear the guilty; visiting the iniquity of the fathers upon the children, and upon the children's children, unto the third and to the fourth generation.'

At this point Yeshua ventured, 'Sir, could that be why one can see destructive behaviour running through families? I've heard that a bullying man in our village had himself been bullied by his father. But he doesn't treat his own family better, knowing how awful it was; instead he's repeating his father's abuse. Also, some beggars maim or blind their children so they only have the opportunity to beg all their lives, rather than working as hired hands. Could that be what the Lord meant about the sins of the fathers being visited upon the children to the third and fourth generation? Sir.'

The Sadducee looked astonished. He had never thought of it like that but it made good sense. Who was this boy?

'Moreover,' the Pharisee said, 'what about when the Lord spoke through the prophet Hosea?

> *'Come, and let us return unto the Lord:*
> *for he hath torn, and he will heal us;*
> *he hath smitten, and he will bind us up.*
> *After two days will he revive us:*
> *in the third day he will raise us up,*
> *and we shall live in his sight.'*

'You've taken that completely out of context!' retorted the Sadducee. 'It's no good just plucking the odd verse or two, here and there, which seem to support your argument, without looking at the whole passage and its historical context. Over a hundred years ago, Jesus ben Sirach wrote that at death a man abides in Sheol, a place of unending sleep and silence. Immortality is restricted to the nation and to a man's good name. Anyhow, we Sadducees believe that only the Torah has divine authority, the rest is commentary.'

'All right then, responded the Pharisee, 'what about when Moses was confronted by the burning bush in Exodus?

> *'God called unto him out of the midst of the bush, and said, "Moses,*
> *Moses". And he said, "Here am I." And he said, "Draw not nigh*
> *hither: put off thy shoes from off thy feet, for the place whereon thou*
> *standest is holy ground. Moreover he said, I am the God of thy father,*
> *the God of Abraham, the God of Isaac, and the God of Jacob." And*
> *Moses hid his face; for he was afraid to look upon God.'*

'The Lord says that in the present tense. Not, "I was the God of Abraham" and so on, but "I *am* the God of ..." so he must mean that in some way Abraham and the Patriarchs are still living. Also, there are all sorts of passages in the Psalms which support the idea of life after death.'

'Well,' said the Sadducee, 'I think you're deluding yourself. Make the best of life while you can, as that's all you've got. There's no point in believing in "pie in the sky when you die". Heavens! Look at the hour. I'd best get going.'

As they rose to leave Yeshua interjected, 'Excuse me Sirs? I wonder if you could explain something to me. I have been studying the Book of Job and he says in one place:

'Man that is born of a woman is of few days, and full of trouble. He cometh forth like a flower, and is cut down: he fleeth also as a shadow, and continueth not … So man lieth down, and riseth not: till the heavens be no more, they shall not awake, nor be raised out of their sleep … If a man die, shall he live again? All the days of my appointed time will I wait, till my change come.

'That seems to suggest that there is no life after death, but there is a later bit which seems to me to imply the opposite:

'For I know that my redeemer liveth, and that he shall stand at the latter day upon the earth: And though after my skin worms destroy this body, yet in my flesh shall I see God: whom I shall see for myself, and mine eyes shall behold, and not another; though my veins be consumed within me.'

'Who is Job's "redeemer"? Is it the Lord or another? I've found this very puzzling.'

The men glanced at each other, then the Pharisee replied, 'Those are interesting and profound questions, which I am afraid neither of us has time now to discuss with you. Perhaps if you came back on another day?'

With that the men left. Yeshua realised he was hungry. His family must be far ahead of him on the road and he couldn't follow now, as it was getting dark. He wandered through the courtyard towards the western gate. He might be able to pick up some falafel down the road but he had no idea where he would stay. He daren't return to the family they had stayed with during Passover, as he'd be in even more trouble.

A gruff but friendly voice addressed him. "'Ere, you OK son?'

Yeshua turned and saw a group of three shepherds also heading towards the gate.

'Well I was hoping to find something to eat. Then I'm not quite sure where I'll stay.'

'Where's your dad?'

'He's gone on ahead with the family and I lost track of the time. I'll catch up with them tomorrow.'

'You're from the north, ain't you, with that accent.'

'Yes I'm from Nazareth, in Galilee.'

'Know what they say about your lot? You can always tell a Galilean, but you can't tell him much!' He chortled at his own joke. 'You can join us if you like. We've a camp just outside the walls, but we'd best get a move on, as they shut the gates at sunset. I'm Jacob by the way, but everybody calls me Jac. This is Nat and that's Andy.'

'Thank you. I'm Yeshua Bar-Joseph.'

They set off westwards, and as they walked, Jac chatted away to Yeshua.

'We're shepherds, but I guess you could've told that from our sheepskin coats.'

Yeshua grinned at him in assent.

'We brought down a load of lambs for Passover, but we've got no work now till the flocks go up to their summer pasture. It's all right for the bosses, but we just get paid by the day. No work no pay.'

Andy struck up a song,

'It's the same the whole world over,
It's the poor what gets the blame,
It's the rich get all the money,
Ain't it all a bleedin' shame.'

'Pleasure,' said Nat.

'What?' asked Andy.

'It's the rich gets all the *pleasure*,' said Nat.

'Amounts to the same thing, money and pleasure,' Andy replied.

They walked on, through the city gate, squinting into the sinking sun, and set off on a dusty road. Jac led the way. He was of average height, leanly built, with unkempt dark hair, a broken nose and a slight squint. He wore old, patched clothes and a sheepskin jerkin, around which he had a thick leather belt with a money pouch attached. It looked pretty full but Yeshua realised it would have to last some time. Jac wore woollen leggings tucked into standard-issue boots. Roman soldier, infantry, for the use of. Yeshua wondered how he'd got them.

'Good boots,' he said.

Jac chortled. 'Yes, I won them off a squaddie at dice. Often wondered how the poor beggar explained that to his centurion.'

They climbed up an escarpment into a quarry and were met by the barking of a huge dog, part shaggy shepherd part Roman mastiff.

'Hello, Fang, old boy!' Jac greeted him, as the dog bounded up, wagging his tail and straining at his chain. The dog wore a spiked collar which made him look extremely fierce, but in fact was to protect him from wolves. 'Been guarding our stuff? Good dog. Andy, could you get the fire going? Nat, get us all a beer would you? The jar's in the back of the cave keeping cool.'

Yeshua glanced around him. A cave had been cut into the limestone quarry side and he realised there were several similar ones nearby. Two had heavy stones at their entrances and another was open and empty like this one. The shepherds had obviously made themselves at home. There were sleeping mats on raised shelves either side of the opening, covered with blankets and a couple of sheepskins. Unwashed plates and drinking cups were piled roughly in a corner, although the top plate looked to have been licked clean. The cave had a pungent smell of damp dog and unwashed human bodies. Yeshua tried not to wrinkle his nose. A fire had been lit at the entrance and still contained a couple of blackened logs, surrounded by lumps of limestone.

Nat handed him a leather mug of beer.

'Cheers!' the men declared, and knocked back their drinks in a few swallows. 'That's good after a dusty day,' said Jac.

Yeshua sipped his more slowly. He had drunk beer before, but not in quantity and he suspected these guys would be drinking for some time. His stomach rumbled.

'Food!' announced Jac. He entered the cave and returned with sheep's cheese, olives and dates. They had brought some fresh bread with them from the city and tore it into hunks before adding cheese. Fang slobbered and was thrown one of the loaves. He gulped it down in seconds. Their discarded cheese rind went the same way. Yeshua realised he was very hungry and they all ate in silence. After more beer and some dates they sat back, feeling better.

'What's your dad do?' asked Jac.

'He's a carpenter-builder. He's got a business with his brother Daniel and they've got a big job on in Sepphoris at the moment.'

'That far from your home?'

'About five miles as the dove flies, but it's over a mountain, so sometimes we stay the night.'

'You working with your dad then?'

'Yes, I've just started.'

''Ere Jac,' said Nat, 'wanna play dice?'

'Why not? Yeshua, you play dice?' Jac asked.

'Er, no. My parents don't approve of gambling,' Yeshua mumbled.

'No harm in a little gamble, it's just a bit of fun. Andy, get us your dice,' said Nat.

Yeshua sighed. 'I don't know how to play.'

'We'll show you,' said Andy. 'We'll play a round, then you can join in.'

'I'd rather just watch.'

'Don't be such a wimp,' said Jac. 'I'll be banker. Andy, get us all another beer along with the dice will you?'

Andy got out three small cubes made from bone. Yeshua saw they had spots painted on each side; one to six.

'The opposite sides all add up to seven,' said Andy. 'So one is opposite six, two, five and so on. Apart from the banker, we all place bets, then the man to the left of the banker throws the three dice together. If they add up to less than ten, the banker wins and takes our stake. If ten or more, the banker pays out the same as each player's stake. It's called "*Tens*" Got it?'

'Think so,' said Yeshua uncertainly.

'We'll play a couple of rounds so you get the hang of it, then you can join in. Got any money on you?' asked Jac.

Yeshua counted. 'Er ... eight *as*.'

'Half a day's pay, not bad for pocket money,' Jac observed.

'Well I am helping my father now,' Yeshua replied, defensively.

'That how you got that scar?' asked Andy, pointing to a nasty fresh weal on Yeshua's left hand.

He nodded. 'Chisel slipped.'

'Right gentlemen,' announced Jac, 'time to place your bets.'

Both Nat and Andy put down two *as*. Nat threw. Two, five and four. Jac grimaced and paid out to each man. Next, Andy bet three *as* and Nat two. Nat threw again. One, three and five.

Jac grinned and scoped up his winnings. He took a swig of beer.

He turned to Yeshua, 'Got it?'

Yeshua smiled weakly and drank some beer. His cup was immediately refilled. He already felt a little woozy but couldn't refuse – he didn't want to be called a wimp again.

'Sit next to me,' said Nat 'you can throw.'

'Gentlemen, place your bets,' intoned Jac.

Yeshua put down two *as*, the others three each. Nat handed him the dice. He sent up a silent prayer asking for forgiveness if the Lord wasn't happy with this. Then he remembered the Book of Job, where the Lord has a wager with Satan, and he felt a bit better. He shook the dice in both hands as he had seen Nat do, and threw. One, six and four. Jac handed him two *as*. He liked that. He placed three *as*, matching the men. He threw again. Three, five and five. Banker loses again. He bet four. Three, four and four.

This is great, he thought. In a few minutes he'd won more than he earned in a day.

Jac looked at him appraisingly. 'Have some more beer.'

'No, I'm fine … Oh all right, thanks.' The beer really was going to his head, but the game was fun.

'You can be banker now,' Jac said. 'Shift round here and I'll throw.'

As Yeshua moved, he thought he saw Jac pulling a different die from his pocket, but it must have been a trick of the light. Fang sighed and snuffled in his sleep.

Jac upped the stakes to five *as*, the others stuck at three. Jac threw. Six, five and four. Yeshua paid out. No matter, he thought, I'll soon win it back and they've given me supper.

Jac bet six, Andy five and Nat four. Jac threw. Six, three and one. 'Bad luck,' said Jac.

'I can't pay you,' said Yeshua, a little alarmed.

'Don't you worry about that son, I'll lend you some. How

about two *denarii*'s worth? That's thirty-two *as*.' Before Yeshua could say a word, Jac had handed them over.

Jac bet six, Andy and Nat five each. Six, two and four. Yeshua paid out again. He'd was sure that the die which came up six was the same one every time, as it was a slightly different colour from the other two. Next time he'd be lucky. Jac bet eight, Nat and Andy six. Six, six and three. The same again and they fell six, one and two. With relief Yeshua scooped up their stakes. Then each bid twelve. Six, three and one. He was cleaned out and owed over two days' wages. How did that happen? he thought in alarm. 'I can't go on,' he said.

'Nice cloak you got there,' said Jac. 'I'll take that in lieu.'

Yeshua reluctantly handed it over. 'I'll just go down the hill a moment,' he said, and walked away from the camp to find a quiet spot in order to relieve himself. He heard the men laugh and felt a little uneasy. But they had seemed so friendly. He looked around. The pale limestone gleamed in the moonlight. There was a faint smell of wild garlic and the distant sound of an owl. The place was deserted. When he'd finished he walked back and heard the men talking in low voices. Something in their tone made him creep nearer, but remain unseen.

'We could sell him to those Gyppos who're going back down south tomorrow,' suggested Andy.

'The ones you met in the camel market?' asked Jac.

'That right's. Gyppos always like young boys,' said Andy.

'As slaves?'

Andy gave a lecherous laugh. 'And the rest.'

'That's disgusting,' Nat interjected.

'What the eye don't see the heart don't grieve over. He'd fetch a good price. You want the money or not?'

Yeshua froze, terrified, then turned and fled down the hill.

'Hang on, he's off!' yelled Nat and sprinted in pursuit. The path was rocky and Yeshua, who had had much more beer than he had ever drunk before, stumbled several times. He was a fast runner and would have got away, but he completely missed the path and plunged headlong into a stream. As he came up choking, Nat grabbed him and held him under to subdue him. They struggled, Yeshua coughing and straining, the pressure growing in his lungs. He felt faint. In despair, fragments of Jonah's prayer came to him. According to the story, Jonah had spent three days trapped in a whale.

> *I cried by reason of mine affliction unto the Lord, and he heard me;*
> *out of the belly of hell cried I, and thou heardest my voice.*
> *For thou hadst cast me into the deep, in the midst of the seas;*
> *.... The waters compassed me about, even to the soul:*
> *the depth closed me round about, the weeds were*
> *wrapped about my head.*
> *… When my soul fainted within me I remembered the Lord*
> *and my prayer came in unto thee, into thine holy temple.*
> *… But I will sacrifice unto thee with the voice of thanksgiving;*
> *I will pay that which I have promised. Deliverance belongs to the Lord!*

Nat dragged Yeshua to his feet, twisting his arms behind him, and marched him up the path back to the cave. As they approached, Yeshua struggled ineffectually. Then he became aware of Fang barking, a couple of flaring torches and a man's voiced raised in anger.

'These are my family tombs! You can't camp here, this is private land!'

Nat and Yeshua rounded the bend and saw a man holding a torch in his right hand, with firelight glinting off the pommel of his sword. He was wearing a hat and a luxurious robe, the quality of which could be discerned even in the semi-darkness. Slightly behind him was a huge Nubian with a torch, brandishing a hefty club.

Jac was grovelling.

'Sorry, your honour. We wasn't to know your honour. No offence your honour.'

Poor shepherds can't afford to get on the wrong side of rich citizens, and the Nubian was immense. Yeshua's heart leaped. He recognised the voice and could now see the men clearly.

'Uncle Joseph!' he shouted, and then started coughing again. 'Uncle Joseph!' he croaked, 'It's Yeshua.'

At this Nat released him and tried to cover their deeds by saying, 'Are you a'right son?' Looking up at Joseph of Arimathea he said apologetically, 'Just fished him out of the stream.'

'Yeshua, what on earth are you doing here? Where are your parents? Why aren't you with them? Never mind that now, you'd better come with me. Don't you have a cloak? You're soaking!'

Yeshua looked over at Jac, who was in shock. He sheepishly handed him his cloak back. They locked eyes; neither of them spoke.

'In the morning I want this whole place cleaned up, with you and that hell-hound out. Do you understand? I'll be sending Shabaka back with some men to check.'

'Yes your honour, of course your honour, we wasn't to know your honour,' Jac muttered, backing away.

Joseph turned and, leading the way, went back down the path followed by Yeshua, with Shabaka taking up the rear. Yeshua started to shiver. It wasn't just that he was wet through, he had his cloak around him now and, though chilly, it wasn't a cold night. He was absorbing the shocking realisation of what had so nearly occurred. He would have disappeared and his parents would never have known what had happened to him. You heard of children disappearing. Occasionally a body was found, but more often they were spirited away, never to be seen again. There was a lively slave trade around the eastern

Mediterranean, occasionally including abducted citizens.

They walked in silence for a while. Then Joseph asked, 'Where are your parents staying?'

'They left today, it's just that I got caught up talking to some rabbis in the Temple and completely lost track of time. They'll have got to Matti's inn, just south of Bethel.'

'Oh, I know the one,' said Joseph. 'They'll probably be coming back tomorrow to find you. I'll send a man to meet them on the way.'

Yeshua was relieved. That was all right then.

'Lucky we met up recently so that you recognised me,' said Joseph. 'If you hadn't been working with your father you might not have known me, although I would have rescued any boy who looked like he was being abducted.'

Joseph had delivered some Lebanese cedar wood to Jo's building project in Sepphoris. He had accompanied it from the port of Tyre down to Acco and then by ox-cart across country.

As they approached the city gate, Yeshua ventured, 'Won't the gate be locked at this time?'

'They'll let *me* in,' asserted Joseph, and indeed they did, with a smart salute from the officer of the watch. Yeshua was impressed. 'Uncle Joseph' was in fact a distant relative, his mother's second cousin; they had mutual great-grandparents. He was a successful merchant, but Yeshua hadn't realised quite how important he must be.

Once inside the walls, they turned right and made their way to the upper city. The streets were narrow with broad, shallow steps, making it easier for donkeys carrying heavy loads to negotiate the slopes. Flaming torches were stuck in brackets on the walls to light the way. On either side the buildings stretched up several storeys, having only small barred windows facing the street, set high up. Even though it was now three hours after sunset there were still people around. Many of them seemed to know Joseph, acknowledging him as they passed. Finally they came to imposing wooden double doors which, when fully opened, would allow a cart through. Set into one of the doors was a more person-sized one, with its own bronze knocker. Joseph struck it once and immediately a small hatch slid open and Yeshua could dimly see a man's peering eye.

'It's us,' said Joseph, and the door swung open. The doorman bowed and, as he straightened up, Yeshua could see surprise in his eyes at the sight of him. Shabaka had to stoop to get through the entrance. The door was bolted firmly behind them.

A pleasant-looking woman bustled up. 'Good to have you back Sir. All's well I trust?'

'Fine, thank you Anna. This is Yeshua. He is the son of Miriam, my kinswoman, who lives in Nazareth. He's had a mishap involving some shepherds and a stream and will be staying with us tonight. He can have Heli's room.'

Heli was Joseph's eldest son who was currently travelling on one of his merchant ships with his brother Janni. 'Perhaps when you've got him warm and dry you could bring him to me in the library.'

'Very good Sir.'

'Have you seen my wife? Is young Rachel still running a fever?'

'Yes she is and Madam is with her.'

'Please let her know I'm home, and will come up to them later.'

'Very good Sir. Now you come with me young man and we'll soon get you toasty.' Anna called to a nearby servant, 'Barny! Bring some hot water for washing and a bowl of broth from the kitchen up to Heli's room.'

The housekeeper led Yeshua across the open courtyard

where a fountain played in the centre, under a colonnade and up some lamp-lit stairs to a first-floor room. It was spacious and had a wooden beamed ceiling interspersed with terracotta tiles. There were large shuttered windows looking out into the courtyard, a comfortable-looking bed, a table and a couple of stools. Anna lit several oil lamps, and Yeshua could see various objects hanging on the walls, but couldn't make them out. A jug of hot water, with a sponge and a linen towel, arrived, along with the broth.

'Now you get those wet things off and sponge yourself down while I find some fresh clothes for you; you're about the same size as Master Janni.'

Yeshua gratefully stripped, poured the water into the washstand, washed and wrapped himself in the towel. He opened the lid of the broth bowl and a delicious smell of lamb and spices greeted him. As he ate, he began to feel a lot better. Anna bustled back. You could hear her coming from some distance as she had an impressive bunch of keys attached to a belt at her waist which clinked as she moved. She laid out fresh clothes and plumped the pillows on the bed. As Yeshua finished eating she said, 'I'll wait outside and once you're dressed I'll take you to the library.'

Shortly afterwards, they set off down the stairs, round to the left under the colonnade, through a heavy oak door decorated with bronze bosses and into a spacious room with a fire burning in the grate. Along one wall there was a latticework of shelving with hundreds of rolls of papyrus slotted into almost all the spaces.

'Come in, come in,' said Joseph. He was sitting in a large chair to one side of the fire and motioned to Yeshua to sit on a slightly smaller one opposite. Joseph was a well-built man in his early forties with flecks of grey already running through his hair and beard. He had the weather-beaten face of a seafarer, with rope-calloused hands. He was dressed in another rich robe, trimmed with fur. Next to him was a flagon and two glasses. He poured Yeshua a modest measure of warm, spiced wine, sweetened with honey.

'Doubt that'll do you any harm,' he said. 'Though I sense you've been drinking beer.' Yeshua reckoned he didn't miss much. 'Now tell me what happened to you.'

Yeshua took a sip of the wine. It was delicious. He had never tasted anything quite like it before. He then drew a deep breath and recounted the evening's events. He concluded by saying he was praying madly as he thought he would drown in the stream.

> *'The waters surrounded me, even to my soul;*
> *The deep closed around me;*
> *Weeds were wrapped around my head.*
> *…Yet You have brought up my life from the pit,*
> *…Deliverance belongs to the Lord!*

'And then, as I was being dragged up the hill, I heard your voice. Truly the Lord is good. He saved me from those who were about to sell me into slavery.'

'Thanks be to the Lord,' concurred Joseph. 'How is your family? I've always been very fond of your mother.'

'Oh they're fine.'

'Come over here,' said Joseph. 'I'd like to show you something.' They stood and went to a long table. Joseph rearranged some oil lamps and Yeshua saw there was a large map laid out, showing lands of which he had never heard.

'We are here.' Joseph pointed to a small strip of land at the eastern end of the sea. 'You see? "Jerusalem".' He pointed to Caesarea. 'My ships' home port is here. In the next week or two Heli and Janni should be getting to the south of Italia and docking in Neapolis. It's Janni's first trip you know. He'll then come back on *Wave Dancer* with a cargo of wine, oil, carpets and bronze cooking vessels. Heli sails on in *Northern Star*, our bigger ship. He's due to go all the way west, through the Pillars of Hercules, here.' Joseph pointed to where the land almost came together at the mouth of the Mediterranean. 'Then they'll turn north and go to Britannia. There he'll buy the finest quality tin, and sell them linen, spices from the East, dried figs and dates as well as the wine he's picked up in Neapolis. Following that, they'll return, trading along the north coast. We hope to have them safely home well before the storm season starts. I should have been sailing with them, but I was negotiating a complex contract to buy some Egyptian granite when it was time for them to leave.'

Yeshua was entranced. All these exotic lands he knew almost nothing about!

'Would you like to travel with us one day?'

Yeshua's eyes shone. 'Wow, that would be awesome, but I've just started working with my father.'

'Well, maybe I can talk to him; who knows? You may develop a talent for trading. You don't have to become a builder you know.' Joseph looked down at the boy fondly; he looked so like his mother. 'Perhaps next year, when you've come of age?' He noticed Yeshua's wound for the first time. 'What happened to your hand?'

'Chisel slipped.'

'Well, we all have to do it once.'

Yeshua grinned wryly.

'Sit down a minute. I'd like to tell you a bit about *my* first voyage.'

They settled in their seats again and Joseph poured himself another glass.

'I accompanied my father on his ship *Leviathan*, when I was about your age. We set off north from Caesarea and hugged the coast. We were carrying cedar wood from Lebanon and some Egyptian linen, as well as papyrus for use in scrolls. Unusually, we had some fine silk fabric which had come overland from the East. We then sailed west along the Anatolian coast and I'll never forget coming into the harbour at Ephesus. It seemed to be lined with white marble, even the streets were paved with marble. When we'd got through the lengthy customs procedures and paid our taxes, we were allowed on shore. The sunlight bounced off the walls and pavements such that we had to shield our eyes. They have a huge temple dedicated to the Roman goddess Diana. Her statue seems to be covered in eggs or pinecones. I'd never seen anything like it. A pilgrim industry thrives on selling silver trinkets of her image. Here's one I picked up there.'

'She does look strange,' said Yeshua. 'Why does she have a deer with her?'

'She is a goddess of hunting, and she could turn people into deer. Well that's according to Greek and then Roman legends. The Greeks call her Artemis.

'We sold some wood and linen there and picked up dried figs, apricots and mulberries, as well as some sweet wine which is particularly good with pastries. We then island-hopped, trading as we went. It's funny, none of the Greek islanders has a good word to say about the residents of any other island. What they say about the mainlanders is unrepeatable! We finished up in the harbour at Athens, Piraeus. Athens is an amazing city, full of ancient monuments. It's a university town, teaming with students and intellectuals from all over the Empire. A melting-pot of ideas. That's where I picked up the first of my scrolls - apart from our scriptures of course. I was introduced to the work of two philosophers called Socrates and Plato. Have you heard of them?'

'I've heard of Plato but I know nothing about what he thought.'

'Their thinking on the nature of reality is more like us Jews than that of the Romans. Their writings seem to imply just the one God, not the plethora of Roman deities. Plato wrote of our reality being like shadows thrown by the light of a fire onto a cave wall. He viewed the spiritual life as being more real than the physical one.'

'Do you believe that?'

'No, we Jews believe that our bodies and spirits are intertwined and are both of importance as the Lord created the bodies of Adam and Eve and breathed his spirit into them.

'Plato was a disciple of Socrates. They lived around the time of the prophet Malachi. Socrates muses on the nature of "good" and "virtue". Not good acts as such, but *underlying* goodness. He proposed that they were transcendent concepts not material ones, so that "goodness" had an authority beyond that of earthly rulers. He mocked the gods of Homeric Greece as not being worthy of worship. Socrates upset his country's rulers, as they considered him a subversive, undermining respect for their authority, especially with impressionable young men. So they put him to death.

'Socrates never actually wrote anything down himself, so we only have Plato's accounts of his philosophy. You should read some, you'd find it interesting and different from our scriptures. Can you read Greek?'

'Yes, but it's a bit basic.'

'Plato is very clear, so a good place to start. Not tonight I think. Now you'd best be getting to bed, I'm sure you've had quite enough excitement for one day.'

'Before I go,' said Yeshua, 'might I go up and visit Cousin Rachel?'

'Well she's running a high fever and it might be catching.'

'I know, but I would like to pray for her.'

Yeshua failed to notice Joseph's raised eyebrow. 'Very well, but we mustn't be long.'

Joseph led the way out along the colonnade and up a second stairwell. As they approached the room, they heard the murmuring of women's voices. Joseph's wife, Ruth, and Anna were there, looking worried. Anna was mopping Rachel's forehead with a damp cloth. The girl was lying in bed, her face flushed, her long dark hair damply splayed across the pillow. Her eyes were shut and she was moaning gently.

'Hello darling. How is she?' Joseph asked.

'No better, as you can see,' Ruth responded. 'Should you have brought the boy?'

'Yeshua has offered to pray for her.'

Ruth glanced at Joseph quizzically but moved aside so that Yeshua could get close to the bed. He picked up a dry hand-towel and put it over his head. Then he placed one hand on Rachel's head and held the other out, palm upwards.

'My heavenly Father; may your name be always be honoured. May your kingdom come here on earth, as it is in Heaven. Please, in your mercy heal Rachel. Take this fever from her and restore her fully. I ask this for your glory, Heavenly Father. Amen.'

'Amen,' echoed the others.

Rachel opened her eyes and looked around, puzzled. The flush faded from her features and she managed a weak smile.

'How are you feeling darling?' her mother asked.

'I, er, I'm feeling fine. Why, what's happening? Hello, who are you?'

She smiled at Yeshua. He smiled back.

'I'm Yeshua Bar-Joseph, we're distant cousins.'

The adults were standing around stunned. Miriam had always implied that there was something special about this boy, but Ruth and Joseph had tended to dismiss it as a mother's first-born-son bias. But, this was amazing! Maybe Miriam had a point.

'I'll stay here a little longer. Rachel you must get some sleep now,' her mother said.

'But I feel fine.'

'Well that's marvellous darling, but it's late and we all need to go to bed.'

Joseph, Yeshua and Anna silently left the room, each going to their own chamber. Yeshua got undressed and put on the nightshirt which had been left folded on the bed for him. He trimmed the wicks of the two oil lamps and then slid beneath the sheets. They were so smooth. He had never felt such finely woven linen before. The blankets were also softer than any they had at home. It must be nice being rich, he thought. But they have worries, just like the rest of us.

Sitting up in bed he raised his hands. 'Thank you Heavenly Father for healing Rachel. Thank you for my deliverance today. Thank you, that when I call on you, you always answer me. Please bless this household and may they sleep in peace. May my parents not worry and keep them safe.'

He blew out the lamps. A thin shaft of moonlight slipped through a crack in the shutters. He slept.

Diana of Ephesus ©Turkish Culture and Tourism office.

CHAPTER 3

Crossed purposes

The sky was just beginning to lighten in the east when Miriam and Jo got themselves together and went down to pick up the donkeys. Rosie and Saffron were surprised to be woken at such an hour and were even more surprised when riding saddles were placed on both of them, rather than baggage packs. Jo and Miriam were taking the minimum of luggage, as they hoped to be back by the following day at the latest. The night watchman, who had yet to be relieved, let them out of the gate and they trotted back down the road towards Jerusalem. Trotting is a comfortable gait for donkeys, less so for their riders, but they wanted to make good time and hoped to be back in the city by midday.

'Remember the first time we came here with Yeshua? When he was only forty days old and we came to redeem him from the Lord?' asked Jo.

'As if I could forget,' replied Miriam. 'Weren't the pair of sacrificial pigeons we bought at the Temple expensive! They must run quite a racket there because, if you bring your own, they say they are blemished and won't do.'

'It's not the only racket. I noticed this week that the commission they charge on changing from Roman to Temple currency and back again was eight per cent each way! Double the norm. If that's not usury, I don't know what is. But I was thinking of that lovely old man Simeon, who took Yeshua into his arms and blessed him. He thanked the Lord that, as he had been promised, he would see the Messiah before he died and that he was now ready to go. That Messiah would be the saviour of both Jews and Gentiles – amazing, and he said it was *our* baby, Yeshua.

'But that wasn't all he said, remember?' added Miriam, 'It's burned into my memory. "Behold, this child is set for the fall and rising again of many in Israel; and for a sign which shall be opposed, so that the thoughts of many hearts may be revealed, *and a sword shall pierce through your own soul too*". Then there was that ancient lady, Anna, who went round the Temple telling anyone who'd listen that baby Yeshua would free Jerusalem from slavery. Well, my soul feels as if it's being pierced at the moment.'

'Yes darling,' Jo replied, 'but the rest hasn't happened yet, so we have to believe that he's all right.'

They continued on in silence, each lost in his and her own thoughts. After a couple of hours Miriam could no longer ignore the stitch in her side brought on by the trotting motion. She was also getting hungry, as they had not yet eaten. They were approaching a wayside inn.

'Shall we stop for a bit?' she said. 'We can ask here if anyone has seen him, and the donkeys could probably do with a drink, I know I could.'

'Yes fine, let's take a break,' Jo replied.

They turned into the entrance and tied up the grateful donkeys, giving them water and some grain. Next to them there was a sweat-stained horse who was still breathing heavily, having been ridden hard. He was a handsome grey, with a fine tooled-leather saddle and bridle, but his rider was nowhere to be seen. Jo went up to the counter to order some cakes and mint infusion.

'You haven't by chance seen a twelve-year-old boy on his own?' he asked.

'No. Why? Have you lost one?' the landlord replied.

'We've probably just mislaid him, but we got separated yesterday when we were leaving Jerusalem and have come back to look for him.'

'Sorry, he's not here.'

'Thanks anyway.'

Jo took the breakfast, went and sat down. Miriam joined him, having gone to wash.

'I asked the servant girl about Yeshua,' she said, 'and she hadn't seen him.'

'No, and I've just checked with the landlord. Wherever can he have got to?'

At that moment a young man emerged with the landlady, bowed to her, mounted the horse and cantered on up the road northwards. Jo couldn't really face his pastry, so Miriam finished it up for him. Shortly afterwards they continued on their way. Sometime later the landlord and his wife got talking.

'Those poor parents,' he said. 'Their twelve-year-old son got separated from them on the journey from Jerusalem and they've lost him. They looked worried sick.'

'Oh no!' said his wife. 'That man on the horse had come looking for them as the boy is with his master, but he's now gone on to Matti's inn. I guess they'll find him soon enough as they must have some idea where he would stay.'

'Yes,' agreed her husband, rather doubtfully.

Progress slowed for Jo and Miriam, as they were travelling against the flow of traffic, with a stream of people leaving Jerusalem, but by midday they had reached the Damascus Gate.

'Excuse me Sir,' Jo addressed the *decanus*, the officer in charge. 'Have you happened to see a twelve-year-old boy on his own? He answers to the name of Yeshua Bar-Joseph.'

'What? We don't run a kindergarten. Now move along, you're blocking the way,' the *decanus* snarled.

They moved along. Roman soldiers were not to be trifled with. They had decided to start in the marketplace but checked the courtyard of the Temple, as it was on the way. Miriam stayed outside with the donkeys while Jo conducted a quick circuit. Not much business was being transacted but there were still several money-changers and dove, sheep and cattle stalls. Yeshua was nowhere to be seen. They carried on to the marketplace.

'We can leave the donkeys for the day at the stables, let's have a bit of lunch and form a plan,' said Jo.

'But he could be anywhere!' wailed Miriam, a note of hysteria in her voice. 'We can eat on the run. Where do we begin?'

Jo spoke with more measured calm than he was feeling. 'I think we should try and be systematic, starting with the market stallholders. We can also send a message to Eleazar in Bethany, asking if he knows anything, and whether we can go back and spend the night with them.'

In the market there were always young boys hanging around who could be hired to deliver messages. Jo picked a fit-looking one, and sent him off to Bethany, giving him some money in advance, promising more on his return and agreeing a meeting time and place. Then they took half the market each, systematically describing Yeshua's appearance and asking the stallholders if they had seen him. No one had. They met on the far side, despondent. Sitting down heavily, they wondered what on earth to do next. By now it was two hours past midday.

★★★

Yeshua awoke to a soft knock on his door.

'Come in,' he said sleepily.

A servant girl entered carrying a jug of hot water and a

towel, which she put next to the washstand. She then opened the shutters and daylight streamed into the room.

'Thanks,' said Yeshua squinting in the sudden light. 'What time is it?'

'Two hours after sunrise,' she replied. 'Breakfast is served in the parlour off the kitchens. Master Joseph said that he has some business in the Temple today and will take you with him, so best get up now.' She said this last with some emphasis.

'Right. Thanks. I'll be down soon.'

In the parlour he found Rachel tucking into bread and honey. Her mother, who had finished eating, was also there.

'Good morning Auntie Ruth. Good morning Cousin Rachel. You look *much* better, how are you feeling?'

'I'm fine. What happened? I sort of remember you coming in to see me last night, but the rest is a bit of a blur,' she asked.

'I'm just pleased you're feeling better,' Yeshua replied and then, keen to change the subject, he asked, 'Auntie Ruth, I understand that Uncle Joseph is to take me to the Temple this morning?'

'Yes, so you'd best not take too long. Here, have some bread and honey. Would you like a hot mint drink?'

'Can I go to the Temple with Papa as well please?' Rachel asked.

'No, you're staying here with me. I need your help embroidering the table linens,' Ruth replied.

'Oh please! It's so unfair! Boys get to do all the interesting stuff. I'll never be allowed to go sailing on Papa's ships or anything,' she wailed.

'Well that's just the way it is,' said Ruth. 'Anyhow, women are said to bring bad luck on ships.'

'Rubbish!' expostulated Rachel. It's just to keep us in our place and out of the way.'

'That's quite enough now!' her mother said sharply. 'Yeshua,

37

if you're ready, Uncle Joseph is expecting you in the library.'

'I'll be off then.' He smiled ruefully at Rachel. 'I know it's unfair. Maybe it won't always be like this.'

Joseph and Yeshua left the house and walked north through the upper city. Herod's palace on the left loomed over the intervening streets. They carried on past the gymnasium and came to the Temple entrance. Joseph turned to Yeshua.

'The old priest Zechariah is on duty this week. They always wheel in the retired priests after Passover, to give the regular clergy a rest,' he said. 'I know his wife, Elizabeth, is a cousin of your mother's, and their son John will be with him. He's about your age, do you know him?'

'Not well, though we met a couple of years ago.'

'I expect you'll get on. He's having some religious instruction from a teacher called Rabbi Nicodemus. I thought you could join them.'

'Thank you Uncle Joseph.'

By this time they had crossed the courtyard, where some of the traders were setting up their stalls, and entered a cool corridor. Joseph stopped at an open heavy wooden door, through which they could hear a man speaking. He knocked and walked in, Yeshua following him.

A man in his late twenties looked up, smiled and walked around a desk to greet them.

'Good morning Master Joseph.' His eyes lit on Yeshua.

'Good morning Nicodemus. I have a new pupil for you today, my kinsman Yeshua. Ah, John, you'll know each other.'

At this a rangy boy, a good half-head taller than Yeshua, came over. He had long dark hair tied in a single plait down his back, deep brown eyes and a serious expression, which softened into a smile as he recognised Yeshua.

Joseph turned to go. 'I'll pick you up from the Temple entrance an hour before sunset. I have various pieces of business to attend to. Do you have any money for food?'

Yeshua looked embarrassed.

'Oh of course not, here you are.' Joseph extracted three small coins from his pouch and handed them over. 'See you later. Learn well.' He nodded towards Nicodemus, turned and left.

'Welcome,' said Nicodemus. 'You'll need to pull up another bench. Could you help him please Simon?'

A stocky boy with a shock of red hair, pale skin and luminous green eyes went over to a bench which was against the wall. He and Yeshua carried it to face the desk. There were a couple of other boys who were holding styluses and wooden boards, coated on the front with soft clay. They wrote by indenting the clay using the stylus. It could be erased with a damp sponge and reused. Papyrus was expensive and only employed for a fair copy.

'John, please will you come and read this passage from the forty-first book of the Prophet Isaiah.'

John picked up an ivory stick which had a hand with a pointing finger carved at its end. He used it to trace the Hebrew, unrolling the scroll with his left hand.

'Comfort ye, comfort ye my people, saith your God.
Speak ye comfortably to Jerusalem, and cry unto her, that her warfare is
accomplished, that her iniquity is pardoned: for she hath received of the
Lord's hand double for all her sins.
The voice of him that crieth in the wilderness, Prepare ye the way of the
Lord, make straight in the desert a highway for our God.
Every valley shall be exalted, and every mountain and hill shall be
made low: and the crooked shall be made straight,
and the rough places plain:
And the glory of the Lord shall be revealed, and all flesh shall see it
together: for the mouth of the Lord hath spoken it.

The voice said, Cry. And he said, What shall I cry? All flesh is grass,
and all the goodliness thereof is as the flower of the field:
The grass withereth, the flower fadeth: because the spirit of the Lord
bloweth upon it: surely the people is grass.
The grass withereth, the flower fadeth: but the word of our God
shall stand for ever.
O Zion, that bringest good tidings, get thee up into the high mountain;
O Jerusalem, that bringest good tidings, lift up thy voice with strength;
lift it up, be not afraid; say unto the cities of Judah, Behold your God!
Behold, the Lord God will come with strong hand, and his arm shall
rule for him: behold, his reward is with him, and his work before him.
He shall feed his flock like a shepherd: he shall gather the lambs with
his arm, and carry them in his bosom, and shall gently lead those that
are with young.'

'So let's look at this text. Now, how do you think the Lord's people have received double punishment for all their sins? John?'

'Could that be when Judah was defeated by the Assyrians and many of our people were taken into exile and then Israel was conquered by the Babylonians and her leading citizens were also exiled in Mesopotamia?'

'Very good John! So where does the "comfort" fit in?'

'Perhaps it refers to the time when the Great King Cyrus allowed our people back to Jerusalem. Would the smoothing of the landscape refer to a road being built between Babylon and Jerusalem?'

'Yes, it may well do. It was a very long time ago. Now Simon, let's see what they teach you in Cyrenaica. Can you think of another passage of scripture where people's short lives are compared with that of grass, which flourishes one day and withers the next?'

'I think it is in a Psalm Sir. The one that starts,

'*Lord you have been our dwelling place in all generations,*
before the mountains were brought forth …

'It goes something like:

'*In the morning people are like grass which groweth up*
and flourisheth, in the evening it is cut down, and withereth.'

'Very good Simon.'

Yeshua raised his hand. 'Please Sir?'

'Yes?'

'Could the smoothing of the landscape also have a spiritual meaning? I wondered if it might be about people's hearts being prepared for the coming of the Lord's messenger. The one who is to declare, "Behold your God!"'

'Where did you get that idea from?'

'I just wondered Sir … Sir, if the Lord is the good shepherd, how will he feed his flock, gather the lambs and lead the young?'

'That's a deep question, Yeshua, and one to which we don't have a definite answer. Many rabbis believe that it refers to the Messiah, the anointed one, who will appear one day to save his people from oppression.'

'Would that be from the Romans? Or could it be the oppression of sin and temptation which turns us away from the Lord, leading him to punish his chosen people?'

Nicodemus' eyes widened in astonishment. Where did this boy get ideas like that from? Metaphorical thought was rare in adults and almost unheard of in a twelve-year-old.

'Another thing Sir? Would the messenger of God in this passage be the same one as the prophet Micah talked of where he said,

'Behold, I will send my messenger, and he shall prepare the
way before me:
and the Lord, whom ye seek, shall suddenly come to his temple,
even the messenger of the covenant, whom ye delight in: behold,
he shall come, saith the Lord of hosts.'

'With which rabbi have you been studying?'

'Rabbi David, in Nazareth, Sir. He thinks that the message of the prophets is both for their time and for some time in the future, when the Lord will free his people.'

'Does he now? And does he also put forward the idea that the messages are spiritual as well as literal?'

'No Sir, in fact if I suggest this he tends to move on in the text.'

Nicodemus smiled. Not a wacky rabbi then, but this boy was disturbing, precocious and interesting in equal measure.

'Well let's see how Rabbi David has taught you to read.'

He rolled up the scroll, placed it carefully on a rack behind him and picked up one several places on. He motioned to Yeshua to start at the beginning of Isaiah 61, and Yeshua read:

'The Spirit of the Lord God is upon me;
because the Lord hath anointed me to preach good tidings
unto the meek;
he hath sent me to bind up the broken-hearted
to proclaim liberty to the captives,
and the opening of the prison to them that are bound;
to proclaim the acceptable year of the Lord,
and the day of vengeance of our God;
to comfort all that mourn;
to appoint unto them that mourn in Zion,
to give unto them beauty for ashes,
the oil of joy for mourning,

*the garment of praise for the spirit of heaviness;
that they might be called trees of righteousness,
the planting of the Lord, that he might be glorified.'*

A shaft of sunlight hit him through a window high in the wall, dust dancing in the rays. His tunic seemed to fluoresce, his hair shone and his skin looked like alabaster, translucent. He stopped reading and an ethereal silence filled the room. The air seemed thick and heavy, as if in a cloud. Nicodemus felt the hairs prickle on the back of his neck. No one moved.

Then Yeshua sat down.

'So what do you make of that, Yeshua?'

'Sir, who is speaking here? Is it the Prophet Isaiah speaking for himself, inspired by the Lord? Or could it refer to the peoples of Israel and Judah, speaking good news to the Gentiles. Or even, might it be another individual we don't yet know about?'

'That is very perceptive of you. It might of course refer to not just one of those, as you were suggesting in the previous passage. Can any of you see how those passages might be linked?'

Yeshua frowned slightly as he pondered this question. Silence. Tentatively he raised his hand.

'Yeshua?'

'Both of these speak of the coming of the Lord's comfort to the suffering. It is as if those who mourn will be comforted, those who are captive, either to others or even to their own inner demons, will be set free. The meek will be blessed. It is as if our world, fallen from the time of Adam and Eve's disobedience, will be restored to the way the Lord meant it to be.'

Nicodemus goggled; then, recovering himself, he said, 'Fascinating. I'd like to meet your Rabbi David some time. That's enough for today boys. Tomorrow I won't be here but you will be privileged to be taught by a very senior priest's son-in-law. He is a fine scholar and will be going places. So you be good for Rabbi Caiaphas. The Lord be with you.'

'And also with you,' chorused the boys.

I'd like to meet that remarkable boy again, thought Nicodemus. I'm beginning to feel he could teach me more than I can teach him.

The boys trooped out into the courtyard, heading for the main gate. Simon turned to the others.

'Fancy a game of football? There's usually one on by the gym.'

They all nodded in assent and joined a small group of boys kicking around an inflated goat's bladder. The rules, if there were any, were fluid, but it was a good way to let off steam. After a while, John said, 'I know a place where we can take lunch. It's cooler than in the city.'

'I'll come,' said Yeshua.

The others resumed their kick-around.

The two of them paused at a roadside stall to pick up some bread pockets stuffed with falafel and sesame paste. John filled his water skin at a fountain. They left the city to the east, through the Golden Gate, and crossed the Kidron valley up to the Mount of Olives. It was cooler here, with a light breeze and the sun filtering though the olive branches, their leaves silvery-green. There would be no actual olives until the autumn. Sitting with their backs against a couple of trunks, they looked towards the city. The valley rose steeply and was topped by the city wall. Beyond it, clearly visible, was the Temple on its mount and the tower of the Antonia Fortress, the headquarters of the Roman Procurator.

'John?' Yeshua ventured.

'Yes?'

'Why do you have such long hair? It's below your waist.'

'That's because I'm a Nazirite. My parents dedicated me to serve the Lord after I was their miracle baby. I was born long after they thought they could have any children. I'm not allowed wine or spirits and I can never marry. My father says an angel spoke to him when he was offering a sacrifice at the Temple one day, and told him that I would be a prophet, preparing the way for the anointed one, the Messiah, who would offer us salvation by forgiving our sins.'

'Awesome!'

'Scary more like!'

'I hope I can marry. I'd like to have kids. I shall call you Naz.'

'Naz? Oh all right then. But I'd heard that you were also a bit of a miracle baby.'

'That's not what everyone's called me. "Bastard" has also been used. Don't know really, but my parents promised to explain matters to me once I've had my bar mitzvah. That was after I found some stuff in a chest.'

'Stuff?'

'My mother asked me to get some linen from her wedding chest, and under all the layers my hand hit something hard. I fished it out and it was a gold casket covered in jewels with a couple of gold coins in it.'

'Wow!'

'Even weirder, next to it was an incense burner, which had never been lit. It contained a lump of incense. It was intricate workmanship, also gold I think. Then there was a box of perfumed ointment. I took so long that my mother came to find me and was horrified at what I had uncovered. I realised they would never have stolen them, but we have nothing else like that in our family. When my father came home they had a conference. They promised that if I said nothing about them to anyone, and didn't ask questions now, they would explain it all when I turned thirteen.'

The sun was high in the sky and a heat-haze rose from the city. The cicadas screeched away. Yeshua saw John reach over and delicately pick one off a branch. He then snapped off its head and popped it in his mouth.

'That's gross!'

'No, they're quite nice actually, specially dipped in honey. Try one.'

'No way!'

'Yeshua, what were you doing yesterday? How did you end up with Master Joseph?'

He recounted the day's events and his hopes that he might be able to sail to distant lands, maybe even as far as Britannia.

They sat in silence for a while, each lost in his own thoughts. Yeshua mused on the scripture they had been reading. Who was this herald who would bring good tidings to Jerusalem? Prophets had a habit of being very unpopular with the ruling classes, as the Lord used them to point out people's wickedness. They usually ended up prematurely dead. He glanced at John. He hoped that wouldn't happen to him. He felt a surge of affection for him and, more surprisingly, for the city. What was that all about?

After a while, John said, 'If you're going to call me Naz, I'd better have a nickname for you. You were the one sheep those shepherds had left to sell. Maybe I'll call you lambkin.'

Yeshua hurled himself at John and they rolled over, wrestling and laughing.

'Lambkin, lambkin, little lost lambkin!' taunted John.

He was stronger than Yeshua and had him pinned to the ground. Then he relented and rolled away.

Sometime later John said, 'We'd best go back, as I'm to meet my father when he comes off duty, and weren't you to be there an hour before sunset?'

'Right,' said Yeshua.

They climbed to their feet.

'Race you to the gate!' shouted John, and set off down the hill.

Yeshua sprinted after him. John had longer legs but Yeshua was fast. John led the way down hill but Yeshua caught up with him halfway up the other side. Finally Yeshua pulled ahead, reaching the gate first. They both collapsed laughing while the guards looked on, unamused. They pulled themselves together and walked back to the Temple. Zechariah and Joseph of Arimathea were already there engaged in conversation with Rabbi Nicodemus.

'Hope we're not in trouble,' said Yeshua, 'I bet I'll get an earful from my parents. They should be here by now. I thought I might see them in the Temple when we got back.'

The men turned as the boys approached.

'Good evening, Uncle Joseph, good evening Rabbi Zechariah, father, good evening Sir,' the boys chorused.

'Hello boys,' said Joseph, smiling, 'The rabbi here has been telling me what an interesting morning you've had. He reckons you two will be teaching him in no time. Just don't get ahead of yourselves.'

The boys looked awkward, but pleased.

Come on Yeshua! Ruth will be expecting us and I expect your parents will be glad to see you.'

'Have they arrived?'

'I'm sure my man will have met them and brought them home. They'll probably have something to say to you.'

'Bye Naz; see you tomorrow?'

'All right Lambkin, unless you've been marched off home. Good to catch up with you. If not, next year in Jerusalem?'

'Next year in Jerusalem,' Yeshua affirmed.

CHAPTER 4

Bethany

Having scoured the market and gone in and out of endless shops, Miriam and Jo returned to the Temple. On the way, they passed a band of Egyptians on camels preparing to leave the city. They had a couple of young boys with them who appeared to be drugged. Approaching the Temple guards Jo enquired, 'Has a twelve-year-old boy been wandering around here on his own?'

'What?' the guard snarled.

'A boy on his own. We got separated yesterday and haven't seen him since. We thought he might have come here.'

'Shouldn't you take more care of your kids? Not just allow them to wander off?'

'Maybe,' said Miriam. 'But have you seen any boy here on his own?'

'Not one I don't recognise.'

'Thanks for your help,' said Jo sarcastically.

'Don't you get clever with me, mister,' the guard retorted.

Jo and Miriam moved into the outer courtyard, where the traders were doing desultory business. Jo went round one way, Miriam the other, asking anyone they met about Yeshua. Unfortunately his description could refer to any number of lads. Nothing. They entered the inner courtyard. Again, nothing. They enquired of a passing priest. No help there either. In despair they stood and prayed together:

'I will lift up mine eyes unto the hills, from whence cometh my help?

My help cometh from the Lord, which made heaven and earth.
He will not suffer thy foot to be moved: he that keepeth thee
will not slumber.
Behold, he that keepeth Israel shall neither slumber nor sleep.
The Lord is thy keeper: the Lord is thy shade upon thy right hand.
The sun shall not smite thee by day, nor the moon by night.
The Lord shall preserve thee from all evil: he shall preserve thy soul.
The Lord shall preserve thy going out and thy coming in from this time
forth, and even for evermore.'

With one last look around they made their way back to the market, and there met the errand boy with Eleazar. Jo thanked the boy and paid him off.

'No sign of him?' asked Eleazar. Though he could tell by their miserable demeanour that there wasn't. 'I've been asking around and heard nothing. Is there anyone in Jerusalem he might have gone to?'

'The only other person is Joseph of Arimathea, who has a house here, but we've never visited it. (He's my second cousin.) Yeshua met him recently on Jo's building project. However, he said he'd definitely not be in Jerusalem this Passover, as he was sailing with his sons, so the house would be shut up, as the rest of his household would be at their country villa. We assumed Yeshua would come back to stay with you,' said Miriam.

'It's too late to look further now,' said Eleazar. 'We'll have to leave town before they lock the gates or they get a bit funny. Not worth getting on the wrong side of the Roman guards. They can make life really difficult.'

They picked up Rosie and Saffron from the stables and made their way through the Golden Gate and out to Bethany, a satellite town of Jerusalem. It was some half an hour's walk through the Mount of Olives. Bethany had a central street and one bisecting it roughly halfway along. A well, which served

49

the entire village with water, stood on one corner of the crossroads, with a rope-pulley and bucket suspended under a wooden roof. Eleazar's house was four down from the well, so his wife, Judith, didn't have to carry water far. The house had a wooden gate opening onto a courtyard and chickens were scratching around, along with a cockerel. This bird had begun crowing on and off throughout the night, and if it didn't stop soon, it was for the pot.

The house was a single storey high and stretched back some way. To its left, within the courtyard, was a covered stable where Eleazar's donkey was tethered. On the left-hand side of the entrance door grew a fig tree, and on the right a grape vine, which had been trained over a wooden frame to give shade to a table flanked by benches. At its head was a carved chair with armrests, with a smaller, armless one at its foot. Several large water jars, one of stone and the others of terracotta, also stood under the canopy. The walls were lime-washed mud brick with an outside staircase going up to the flat roof.

Jo stabled the donkeys, un-tacked them, filled their water buckets and put a large bunch of clover in each manger. He gave them each a quick brush down, sending clouds of dust into the air. Sneezing several times, he left them munching contentedly.

The front door opened onto a large living room with a fireplace in the right-hand wall, surrounded by couches. It could get cold in the winter. The kitchen was off to the left, where Miriam was already helping Judith. Straight ahead, an opening led onto a corridor off which were several bedrooms.

As Jo entered, Eleazar handed him a beaker of red wine mixed with a little water.

'I imagine you'll need this,' he said.

Jo downed it in one, then looked a bit embarrassed, but Eleazar wordlessly refilled it. They reclined on the couches. At that moment Martha, Eleazar's eldest, aged ten, came through carrying plates topped by a salad bowl.

'Good evening Uncle Jo. I understand you've lost Yeshua,' she declared.

'We think we'll find him tomorrow.'

'Have you checked in the marketplace and in the Temple?' Martha asked. 'Could he be with anyone else? Why wouldn't he have come back here?'

Jo had got used to her directness and logic, but it was still a bit disconcerting coming from a girl so young. He thought she had all the makings of an excellent project manager, but would only ever have the opportunity to manage her household.

'Mary-Beth, could you stop playing now and help me lay the table.' Martha addressed her younger sister who was sorting out her Noah's Ark animals into pairs. There were sheep and camels, cows, horses, dogs, bears, doves and ravens. All were of painted wood and Noah, his three sons and their wives completed the collection. They could just fit into the Ark if you took the red roof off and packed them carefully. The Ark had several portholes, a door in one side, which opened and closed, and a little wooden ramp down which the animals could process.

'I'm busy.'

'No, you're just playing. Please stop. Papa! Tell her to stop playing and help me.'

'Oh leave her alone, just this once,' Eleazar responded.

'But that's not fair! Why do I always have to do everything?'

'Enough!' said her father, 'just get on with it.'

Martha stomped off, crashing the plates down on the courtyard table and then banging earthenware beakers together, such that they were in danger of chipping.

'Who'd have daughters?' laughed Eleazar, 'but they do help Judith. However,' he lowered his voice but Mary-Beth appeared to be taking no notice, 'we do so long for a son, but no sign of one yet.'

'Judith's still young,' said Jo. 'I'm sure the Lord will bless you in time.'

'Let's hope so.'

'Supper's ready,' called Judith. 'Wash your hands please children and come and sit down.'

She emerged carrying a large pan of baked, beaten eggs, flavoured with onions and herbs. Miriam followed with bread on a wooden board and a fearsome looking knife. Eleazar sat in the large chair, with Jo and Miriam either side of him. The girls were next to them with Judith opposite her husband. Eleazar lifted his hands and bowed his head. The others followed.

'Lord, thank you for this food. Please bless us who eat it, bless those who will go hungry tonight and please keep Yeshua safe and may we find him tomorrow, Amen.'

'Amen,' intoned the others.

Judith cut the egg dish into wedges and passed the plates up the table. She then sliced the loaf and indicated that they should take bread and salad. Eleazar poured watered wine for everyone, and further diluted it for the children. It was a bit safer to drink than water on its own, but no one knew why.

Suddenly Miriam exclaimed, 'I think we should try and find Joseph. What if he didn't go sailing? He might be in Jerusalem. How could I have been so stupid not even to try? Jo, why didn't *you* think of that?' Her voice rose higher as she turned accusingly to her husband.

He thought fast and said, 'Well I've done business with him, and I know you spent time together when you were younger, but we don't know him well and I've no idea where he lives. I can't believe Yesh would end up there. Eleazar, do you happen to know where Joseph of Arimathea lives?'

'Sorry, no, I've never heard of him.'

'He's a rich merchant,' Miriam interjected.

'Then I imagine his house would be in the upper city. I've done some work there and could ask around tomorrow.'

'But we must go back there tonight!' shrieked Miriam, and then struggled to keep her voice under control as she saw the startled faces of the children. 'It's not far.'

'They lock the gates at sunset,' Martha announced. 'You have to have a good reason for them to let you in after that. And you have to bribe them.'

Her father looked embarrassed. How had she picked that up? She was a bright girl and no mistake. Just a pity she wasn't a boy.

'We can't go back now,' said Jo, 'and he isn't likely to be moving around at night. We'll go back first thing tomorrow.' Again he sounded calmer than he felt.

Miriam picked up another piece of bread, dunked it into the oil and vinegar salad dressing and ate it nervously. She thought, whatever can have happened to him? Had he been abducted? After all, dreadful things happened to men who were chosen by God. Most of the prophets came to untimely ends. Then there was the historical Joseph, the one with the multi-coloured coat. He was sold by his jealous brothers into slavery in Egypt and his father thought he was dead for at least twenty years. What could he have gone through during all that time? What if they never found Yeshua?

That night Miriam tossed and turned. She slept fitfully and dreamt of Yeshua being sold as a slave. Whatever the prophecies concerning him, she might never see him again. She woke in a sweat and silently yelled at the Lord,

My God, my God why hast thou forsaken me?
Why art thou so far from helping me and from the

words of my groaning?
O my God, I cry in the daytime but thou hearest not;
and in the night season and am not silent.

Jo also had a disturbed night; apart from Miriam's restlessness, that wretched cockerel kept starting up. Why hadn't anyone strangled it yet?

CHAPTER 5

Crossed swords

Yeshua woke early and opened the shutters. He was fascinated by Heli's trophies hanging on the wall. There was a Berber scimitar which had a curved blade in a scarlet leather scabbard decorated with silver. The hilt was ivory, also inlayed with silver. Yeshua lifted it down from the wall and unsheathed it. The tempered steel was razor-sharp. He swished it to and fro, then whirled it around his head. It wasn't as heavy as the Roman legionaries' short swords, and was far more elegant. He sheathed it and carefully hung it up again. Next to it there was an alabaster block with an outline that looked a bit like a Roman stadium. It had a rounded top and bottom with straight sides. Inside it were carved a circle with a dot in its centre, a sceptre topped with a jackal's head, a seated goddess topped with a feather, an adze, a wavy line, and another dotted circle. A piece of papyrus lying next to it explained that this was the cartouche containing the throne name of Pharaoh Ramesses II - the Pharaoh who ruled Egypt when the Lord commanded Moses to lead his people out from slavery and into the Promised Land. There was also a large, oval bronze shield with swirling patterns embossed on it, attached to a wooden back. It was quite different from the Roman curved, rectangular design or even those of the Temple guards. He wondered from where it had come. Lifting it down, he found a piece of papyrus tucked into its hand-grip which had written on it, 'A shield of the Cornovii tribe from southwest Britannia'.

Would his father allow him to sail with Uncle Joseph? With

a jolt he realised that his parents didn't actually know where he was. But that was all right, as he was off to the Temple again this morning and they were bound to come looking for him there. They knew his devotion to the scriptures and his hunger at learning their interpretation. He felt very close to the Lord and was sure of his guidance. He covered his head, raised his hands and recited Psalm 147:

> 'Praise ye the Lord: for it is good to sing praises unto our God;
> for it is pleasant; and praise is comely.
> The Lord doth build up Jerusalem:
> he gathereth together the outcasts of Israel.
> He healeth the broken in heart, and bindeth up their wounds.
> He telleth the number of the stars; he calleth them all by their names.
> Great is our Lord, and of great power:
> his understanding is infinite.
> The Lord lifteth up the meek:
> he casteth the wicked down to the ground.
> Sing unto the Lord with thanksgiving;
> sing praise upon the harp unto our God.'

Shortly afterwards the servant girl knocked softly and brought in his washing water.

Joseph was breakfasting with the family. As Yeshua entered, he said, 'My man missed your parents yesterday. He caught up with your Aunt Hannah who told him that they had returned to Jerusalem. I'm sure we'll meet up with them today. The city isn't that big and it's emptying of visitors fast. I'll leave a message for them in the marketplace as well as at the Temple. Do you know where they will have stayed last night?'

'Possibly in Bethany, where we stay over Passover. Eleazar used to be a neighbour in Nazareth, but moved down south, as there was more work for a stonemason in Jerusalem. The

Temple always seems to need repairing.' Yeshua said this while helping himself to bread and honey. He had noticed that much of Joseph's house was stone-built, in marked contrast to his parent's mud-brick one.

'If we haven't caught up with them by midday, perhaps you should go to Bethany and see. We leave for the Temple shortly. I gather Caiaphas will be teaching you today. Rumour has it that his father-in-law, Annas, will be our next High Priest.'

As they left the house Yeshua noticed for the first time that the courtyard contained several large earthenware pots containing apricot trees and others with lemon trees. Apricots were a real delicacy which he'd never eaten.

As they walked Joseph said, 'I'm sure you'll meet up with your parents today, but they must be worried.' Yeshua remained silent. He wasn't quite sure what his reception would be once his parents arrived.

They entered the same room as the day before where the other boys were already assembled. Behind the desk stood a slim young man with a long, thin face, lank, dark hair and the coldest grey eyes Yeshua had ever seen. He smiled thinly at Joseph and glanced at the boy.

'Good morning Rabbi Caiaphas. This is Yeshua Bar-Joseph whom I think Rabbi Nicodemus will have mentioned.'

'Indeed. He seemed very impressed with him. We'll see how he gets on today.'

Joseph left and Caiaphas indicated that Yeshua should sit on the bench next to Simon.

'We are looking at a passage from the book of the Prophet Samuel today. Simon, would you come and read it for us? 1 Samuel, Chapter 2 starting at verse 12.' Simon read:

'Now the sons of Eli were corrupt; they did not know the Lord. And the priests' custom with the people was that when any man offered a *sacrifice, the priest's servant would come with a three-pronged meat-hook in his hand while the meat was boiling. Then he would thrust it into the pan, and the priest would take for himself all that the meat-hook brought up. So they did in Shiloh to all the Israelites who came there. Also, before they burned the fat, the priest's servant would come and say to the man who sacrificed, "Give meat for roasting to the priest, for he will not take boiled meat from you, but raw." And if the man said to him, "They should really burn the fat first; then you may take as much as your heart desires," he would then answer him, "No, but you must give it now; and if not, I will take it by force." Therefore the sin of the young men was very great before the Lord.'*

'John, what was the problem with Eli's son's behaviour? Also, can you think of anyone else in the scriptures who behaved similarly?'

'Well instead of just taking from the pot of sacrificial meat that which their forks would bring up, they wanted the best cuts before they had been offered to the Lord. This meant that the man offering his sacrifice to the Lord would not be giving his best quality meat, but only whatever the priests rejected. Could it be a bit like Abel, who offered the Lord his finest lamb, thereby pleasing the Lord, as distinct from his elder brother Cain, who offered second-rate produce, which he thought would be "good enough". Only the Lord saw into Cain's heart, that he valued himself more highly than he did the Lord, and so he didn't accept his offering.'

'Very good John. Of course priests nowadays never behave like Eli's sons. We are scrupulous to keep all of the Lord's commands. Each of us tithes our quota of money, herbs and spices. We keep all the purity laws and never miss a holy day.'

'Please Sir,' ventured Yeshua.

'Yes?' said Caiaphas, slightly annoyed. He wasn't used to boys taking the initiative.

'Sir, I can't help noticing that all our priests are really well fed and dressed, whereas there are lots of ragged, hungry beggars at the Temple entrance. Didn't the Lord command justice and mercy, along with tithing, as paths to the Kingdom of Heaven?'

Caiaphas' eyebrows shot up. Who was this boy who dared to impugn the honesty and probity of the priesthood?

'Anything else you'd like to share with us Yeshua?' he asked sarcastically and, he hoped, rhetorically.

'Well actually, as the Lord sees into our hearts, why do priests make such a great show of praying on street corners and wearing extra-long shawl fringes and large phylacteries which must be impractical, not to say uncomfortable. If the Lord knows how holy they are, why do they do that? Is it to impress the rest of us Sir?'

Caiaphas, breathing heavily, was about to respond.

'Another thing, Sir,' continued Yeshua heedlessly, 'scripture says that the Lord's Temple should be a house of prayer for all nations. The only place Gentiles are allowed to worship is in the outer court, but what with all those souvenir stalls, animals and money-changers, it's more like a circus. No one could pray in that racket.'

Caiaphas felt he was about to explode.

He thought, how dare this little northern nobody, with his uncouth regional accent, criticise the Lord's chosen priesthood and how we run the Temple? We, who were set apart from the time of Moses to serve the Lord, and were to be provided with all our needs by the rest of the tribes, having no land of our own.

Before he could speak, there was a knock on the door which immediately opened and Yeshua's parents entered. Miriam rushed over to him, almost bodily lifted him off the bench and hugged him. Then she started shouting.

'How could you go off on your own like that! We've been worried sick. You've been gone for days. Anything could have happened to you. How could you be so stupid? Don't you have any consideration for other people? We've had to leave James and little Sarah with Hannah and borrow their donkey. You're so thoughtless!'

It seemed to Yeshua to go on and on. During this outburst, Jo went up to Rabbi Caiaphas and apologised for bursting in as they had. They had only just learned where Yeshua was and they had been searching for him since the day before yesterday. The other boys were entranced by this diversion. Judging by the look on Caiaphas' face, Yeshua was in line for a beating, so his parents had turned up in the nick of time. This was the most exciting lesson they had ever had.

Finally, order was restored, and Miriam marched Yeshua out. Jo apologised again, smiled at John, and caught up with mother and son halfway across the courtyard. Caiaphas looked after them, white with anger. He hoped *he'd* catch up with that precocious little smart-arse one day. Then he'd teach him some manners and a proper respect for the Temple and its priesthood.

'Class dismissed. The Lord be with you.'

'And also with you,' the boys chanted in unison.

As they left the Temple, Miriam started up again.

'How could you have gone off like that? Your father and I have been worried sick and been searching for you everywhere.'

'But you must have known where I'd be. I'd be bound to be in my Heavenly Father's house. It feels like where I belong.'

'You weren't here yesterday afternoon!' interjected Jo.

'Er, no, lessons were over and I went up the Mount of Olives with John. But I was quite safe, and Uncle Joseph sent a messenger to meet you and bring you to his house. Have you ever been there? It's huge. He must be very rich and he wants to take me on a trading trip. Please can I go?'

As soon as he uttered this he realised it was probably not quite the best moment to ask a favour. Oh well, he'd said it now.

'We weren't to know that you were all right!' Miriam continued. 'We're going to Joseph's house now. He'd left a message at the Temple gate that we should join them for an early lunch. We'll get back to Matti's before nightfall.'

Yeshua was pleased that he wasn't leaving Jerusalem without saying a proper goodbye to Uncle Joseph and Auntie Ruth. And, to his surprise, he was also pleased that he would be seeing Rachel again. Up until now he had never had much time for girls, but she had a most beguiling smile.

By the time they arrived, lunch had been laid out under the colonnade. Their donkeys had been collected from the market stables and were at the back, munching, next to several rather fine horses.

Joseph sat at the head of the table flanked by Jo and Miriam. Yeshua was next to his mother, opposite Rachel, with Shabaka on his left and Ruth at the other end. The conversation flowed, though the atmosphere was somewhat stilted. During a lull, Yeshua asked, 'Uncle Joseph, I was wondering, in Heli's room there is a seated statue of a fellow in a pleated robe with a top-knot, dangly ears and a dreamy expression on his face. Who's that?'

'Oh I can tell you,' said Rachel. 'Heli explained him to me. He comes from India over in the East and he is called Buddha. There, they have lots of gods like the Greeks and the Romans. Apparently, he was a prince who lived hundreds of years ago. One day he got out of the palace and saw a beggar and a starving man. He realised that not everyone was as fortunate as he was, and decided that our problems were caused by us wanting stuff. If we could let go of all our attachment to things and to people we would be content. He called it enlightenment.

He lived the life of a wandering rabbi, relying on people's charity for food and shelter. He attracted a large following of disciples and is viewed by them now as half philosopher-half god.'

'That's really interesting, thanks,' said Yeshua warmly. 'I can understand the problem with being too attached to things, if you just want more and more money; but giving up on people as well, that seems very self-centred. As if the Lord didn't exist and our own happiness was all that mattered.'

'Well that's who that is,' concluded Rachel, with a smile, which Yeshua returned. He then turned to Shabaka.

'Might I ask you a question?'

A smile lit up the Nubian's face as he looked down at the boy. 'Certainly.'

'I was wondering about the significance of the lion-headed-man amulet you wear around your neck?'

'It represents our god of war, Apedemak. He is associated with the Nubian royal line, as am I. I believe in your Jewish faith, Jacob's son Judah was compared with a lion, and he was an ancestor of King David. Am I right in thinking that you are of the house of David?'

Yeshua assented. 'Yes you are. Thank you. Are you interested in our faith?'

'Indeed. As I have lived in this household I have seen how it informs every aspect of the lives and works of this family and of others. Your god is a powerful god, gracious and merciful; slow to anger, and abounding in steadfast love, seemingly ready to relent from punishing. However, some of your religious rules and regulations remain a mystery to me.'

'You and me both. However, I pray that one day you will know our Lord as a loving father, as I do,' said Yeshua. He then became aware of a faint aura of awkwardness around the table.

At that moment Shabaka excused himself, as he had some business to attend to. Once he was out of earshot, Miriam asked, 'Isn't it unusual for your servants to eat with you?'

'Oh, Shabaka isn't a servant,' said Ruth. 'Years ago he saved Joseph's life. He belonged to an Egyptian, who had bought him in the slave market at Thebes and brought him to Alexandria. He'd been captured by a raiding party on the Egyptian border when he was about fifteen years old. His master found that he was bright and honest, so had him taught to speak and write Greek. When Shabaka rescued Joseph, he was in charge of stores on his master's vessels. Joseph managed to persuade his father's agent in Alexandria to redeem and free him. Shabaka joined Janni's business and was made a partner in it some years ago.'

'Amazing!' said Miriam, 'I've never come across the name Shabaka before.'

'He told me he's named after a Nubian who became pharaoh over all of Nubia and Egypt, before the time of our exile,' responded Ruth.

The meal over, Jo, Miriam and Yeshua took their leave of Joseph's family.

The atmosphere on the way back started frosty. Yeshua was affronted that his parents hadn't known he would be at the Temple and were still treating him like a little boy. He conveniently glossed over the fact that he had almost come to grief at the hands of the shepherds. He marched on ahead of the donkeys, shoulders stiff and head held defiantly high. Miriam rode Rosie and Jo, Saffron. They had a neat pack of Yeshua's clothes which had all been laundered and pressed, much to Miriam's embarrassment. Janni's tunic, which Yeshua was wearing, was made of finer quality linen than they could have afforded.

Somehow they had picked up the story that Yeshua had

temporarily lost his cloak playing dice. Jo called him back to raise the matter.

'Haven't we told you not to gamble? Apart from the fact that you can lose your shirt, which you seem to have found out, it can become addictive. Men have been ruined thinking they'll make it all back on the next throw. Besides, scripture forbids it.'

'What? Well what about Job? The Lord makes a wager with Satan that Job will remain faithful despite misfortune, remember?'

He started to quote. He really had the most remarkable memory for scripture.

'There was a man in the land of Uz, whose name was Job; and that man was perfect and upright, and one that feared God, and eschewed evil … Now there was a day when the sons of God came to present themselves before the Lord, and Satan came also among them. And the Lord said unto Satan, Whence comest thou? Then Satan answered the Lord, and said, From going to and fro in the earth, and from walking up and down in it. And the Lord said unto Satan, Hast thou considered my servant Job, that there is none like him in the earth, a perfect and an upright man, one that feareth God, and escheweth evil?

Then Satan answered the Lord, and said, Doth Job fear God for nought? Hast not thou made an hedge about him, and about his house and about all that he hath on every side? Thou hast blessed the work of his hands, and his substance is increased in the land. But put forth thine hand now, and touch all that he hath, and he will curse thee to thy face. And the Lord said unto Satan, Behold, all that he hath is in thy power; only upon himself put not forth thine hand. So Satan went forth from the presence of the Lord.'

Miriam exploded, 'Who do you think you are then? Satan or God?'

Yeshua stormed off again, failing to see Jo and Miriam look at each other as parallel shivers slithered down their spines.

Gradually, Yeshua realised he really had to apologise to his parents. Slowing his pace, he dropped back until he was walking between the heads of the donkeys. He stroked Rosie's velvety muzzle, steeling himself, not yet sure what to say. Rosie rubbed her head on his shoulder affectionately, and blew out of her nostrils. Jo and Miriam glanced at each other and smiled, waiting.

Staring stolidly forwards, Yeshua took a big breath and said, 'I'm sorry I wandered off when we were leaving. I didn't mean to be so long but I just lost track of the time. I realise now that I put you to a lot of trouble and that you must have been very worried. I won't do it again, I promise.'

'That's all right son,' Jo responded, 'but we *were* very worried and you must admit things could have turned out far less well than they did.'

'Yes, I know, I'm sorry.'

'We'll say no more about it but please never do it again.'

Having made their peace, Jo recounted the most extraordinary story he had heard in the marketplace.

'A man was going down from Jerusalem to Jericho and fell among thieves. They stripped him and beat him and left him half dead. Various people passed him but no one went to see if he needed help.'

'Well I suppose they didn't want to be contaminated if he'd been dead,' said Miriam. 'Imagine if a priest had touched him, he would have had to go all the way back to Jerusalem to purify himself before setting out again.'

'Well I gather that a priest and a Levite both ignored him, but guess who went to help?'

'No idea. Go on, tell us.'

'A Samaritan!'

'A what!' Yeshua and Miriam exclaimed simultaneously.

'But we Jews don't have anything to do with Samaritans,' said Miriam.

'Yes I know, extraordinary isn't it? I know it was true because the innkeeper who took them in told me so himself. Moreover, the Samaritan paid for the victim's care and said he would settle any further costs incurred on his return journey.'

'Why do we hate the Samaritans?' Yeshua asked.

'Lots of reasons,' said Jo. 'For a start they aren't native to these parts, but were transported here by Assyrians hundreds of years ago.'

'How long do you have to live somewhere before you can be considered a native then?' asked Yeshua.

'Don't interrupt! They also harassed us when we were rebuilding the Temple after it had been destroyed. And then they attacked us when Nehemiah was rebuilding Jerusalem's walls. Moreover, when Judas Maccabee was throwing out the Greeks, a Samaritan general who had adopted a Greek name, Apollonius, attacked Judas, but was beaten back. Most recently, Herod's a bit too chummy with them; as you know, he's not really Jewish either.'

'Looks like this Samaritan understood the command in Leviticus about loving your neighbour as yourself better than we do. He must have known that if the roles had been reversed no Jew would have helped *him*, after all they wouldn't even help a fellow Jew, just in case it inconvenienced them!' Yeshua said, both admiringly and disapprovingly.

Again, he walked on ahead, but this time not in a strop.

Miriam dropped her voice and said to Jo, 'I can't forget

those words of Simeon, "and a sword shall pierce through your own soul too". These last few days have been like a permanent sword through my soul. I cannot imagine a worse three days of my life, ever.'

Cartouche of Ramesses II

First century British shield ©The Trustees of the British Museum

Seated figure of the Buddha, Gandhara
© Government Museum and Art Gallery, Chandigarh, India

PART 2

JERUSALEM,
21 YEARS LATER

CHAPTER 6

Betrayal – Thursday night

Yeshua saw through the trees the line of torches snaking down from the city walls. He reckoned he had half an hour before they arrived. Fear gripped his bowels. He'd left most of his companions a little distance away and gone up with Peter, and the Zebedee boys, to pray. They'd instantly fallen asleep. Well, it had been a good dinner with a lot of wine. He, on the other hand, had gone slightly further off and thrown up. In fact his entire digestive tract had emptied itself in a rush. At least he wouldn't disgrace himself in that way later. He was sweating profusely, yet felt icy cold. He had never felt so alone. Even his Heavenly Father, who throughout his life had always been so near, appeared to have deserted him. He prayed, 'Father, you can do anything. Take this cup from me. Spare me this terrible fate.'

He felt nothing. He looked up at the pitiless, star-studded sky, with a full moon rising.

Nothing. Then he remembered himself.

'Father, not what I want but what you want.'

Still nothing. He felt detached from every living creature, as if he were on another planet. Totally disconnected. Disengaged. Everything was pointless, meaningless, an aching void. No one cared about him. His closest friends just slept. Even when he woke them and asked them to stay with him, they immediately dropped off again. The spirit is willing but the flesh is weak, he thought.

Terror gripped him. There was no escape. Time stood still

yet sprinted on. The torches had arrived at the valley's base and were beginning to climb the slope towards him.

'My God, my God, why hast thou forsaken me?
why art thou so far from helping me, and from the words of my
groaning?
O my God, I cry in the daytime, but thou hearest not;
and in the night season, and am not silent.
But thou art holy, O thou that inhabitest the praises of Israel.
Our fathers trusted in thee: they trusted, and thou didst deliver them.
They cried unto thee, and were delivered:
they trusted in thee, and were not confounded.
But I am a worm, and no man; a reproach of men, and despised of the
people.
All they that see me laugh me to scorn:
they shoot out the lip, they shake the head saying,
He trusted in the Lord that he would deliver him:
let him deliver him, seeing how he delighted in him.'

Now he could hear them. Soon they would be upon him. He pulled himself together, went to the others and said, 'Are you still asleep? Look, it's time and I'm betrayed. Get up! Here come Judas and the others.'

At that moment a group of Temple guards burst upon the companions. They were heavily armed with swords and clubs. Judas stepped forward and said, 'Master!'

He kissed Yeshua, at which sign two of the party grabbed him, one of whom was Malchus, the High Priest's slave. Peter leaped to his defence, slicing off Malchus' ear with his sword. But Yeshua shouted, 'Enough! Peter, put up your sword.' Then he turned to the guards. 'Why have you come to arrest me in the dead of night armed to the teeth? Every day I was in the Temple and around town. You could have invited me in. Am I an armed robber?'

He picked up the ear and replaced it, leaving it fully healed.

The guards said nothing, but secured Yeshua and went to arrest some of his disciples, although that was beyond their remit. But they had disappeared into the darkness, apart from one young man whom they grabbed by his tunic, but he struggled free and fled, naked.

The arresting party returned to the city and took Yeshua to the house of the High Priest, Caiaphas, where his father-in-law Annas and selected elders of the Temple had assembled. Two of Yeshua's disciples, Peter and Philetus, followed at a distance. On arrival Philetus caught up with the party and entered the courtyard, as he was well known there. He realised Peter had been stopped at the gate, so he spoke to the doorkeeper, who let him in. Peter mingled with the servants standing round a brazier.

While Peter was below in the courtyard, one of the High Priest's servant girls came by. She saw Peter warming himself, stared at him and said, 'You were with Yeshua, the man from Nazareth.'

'Nonsense! I don't know who you're talking about.'

He moved away into the forecourt. In the distance a cock crowed. The servant-girl then insisted to the bystanders, 'He's definitely one of them.'

But again he denied it. After a little while another man said to Peter, 'Of course you're one of them; you've got a Galilean accent.'

Peter swore. 'For God's sake! I've never damn well seen him before!'

At that moment the cock crowed again. Yeshua, who was being held some way off, turned and caught Peter's eye. With an awful sinking sense of realisation, Peter remembered that Yesh had said to him, 'Before the cock crows twice, you will deny me three times.'

He broke down and ran, weeping.

CHAPTER 7

Naked truth – Thursday night

Lazarus fled naked down the hill. He must get home and warn the others, he thought. Thank heavens Bethany was on this side of the city. He ran parallel to the road. It was unlikely he'd meet anyone at this hour, but just in case. He could see well enough in the moonlight, but still stumbled several times, once falling flat on his face, totally winded. He recovered and set off again, finally turning into Bethany's main street. Immediately the dogs started up. No discreet homecoming then. As he approached his gate, his immediate predicament became clear. He was naked. Now it was all very well for those Romans to go prancing around starkers in the gym and the baths, but Jews were never uncovered. Ever since Noah's son Ham had been cursed by his father for having seen him drunk and naked and not covered him up, Jews were very modest about their private parts. And here he was, just in sandals. Even worse, he knew the house was full of women. Yeshua's mother and Mary Magdalene, known as Magda, were staying with his sisters, Martha and Mary-Beth. Hard to know whom it would be worst to meet. No help for it. He banged on the gate. Shortly afterwards he saw the front door open and the silhouette of Martha approaching.

'It's me. Let me in quick,' he hissed.

She opened the gate and hardly knew where to look. Having briefly checked that he seemed unhurt, Martha dropped her gaze. At least he still had his sandals. She had never seen a man naked and hadn't seen Lazarus so since he was seven years old, ten years ago. He shot past her through the living room and into his chamber, where he flung on a robe. Then the donkey started up,

'HEE AAW HEE AAW HEE AAW AWW AWW AWW.'

Well that will have woken the entire village, thought Martha. Now what on earth has happened?

Lazarus entered the living room as the others came sleepily out of their chambers. Martha firmly re-bolted the door.

'They've taken Yeshua!' he blurted.

'Who?' Miriam asked, her eyes widening in alarm.

'The Temple guards, they came to Gethsemane and arrested him.'

'I told you to come back with us,' said Martha crossly, 'but *no*, you insisted on going off with the men and now look at you.'

'Leave him alone,' said Mary-Beth 'we can't keep him a boy forever.'

'It's not that,' replied Martha, 'he's been a marked man ever since Yeshua brought him back from the dead. It's like his presence is a permanent reminder to the priests of who Yeshua might really be. Did they try to arrest you too?'

'Yes. They just got my tunic.'

'You see! Did they pick up any of the others?'

'I don't know. I just ran as fast as I could.'

Miriam broke in, 'We must go into town now. We can't just leave him there, and they won't arrest us women. They're much easier about letting you in and out of the gates over Passover than in the past.'

'All right,' said Martha, 'but Lazarus, you are to stay here. We need someone to be at home in case any of the others seek sanctuary. For once, you can be in charge.'

Lazarus grimaced, but knew it was no good arguing. He doubted he would ever be in charge until he married, and even then he was not so sure. Rules and reality did not always coincide. He remembered his father commenting, more than once, that Martha would have made a great project manager, and that Yeshua's father, Jo, had thought so too. Pity *he* seemed to be her principal project at present.

The women prepared to leave, each hoping that the donkey wouldn't start up again.

'We ought to go to back to John-Mark's house to see what they know,' said Martha, handing out flaming torches to the others. That was where they had all had supper earlier that evening. Mercifully, the donkey remained silent. Nothing one could do about the dogs though.

Lazarus locked up and then didn't know what to do with himself. Sleep was out of the question. He had a bit of a wash and stoked up the fire in the kitchen, putting some water on to heat. If anyone was brought here wounded that might be useful. He paced the floor, his thoughts whirling. What if they did arrest the women, what would he do then? And Yesh, he loved him so much. Yesh had been like a big brother to him. He'd known him all his life, as his family always stayed with them over Passover. And he'd brought him back from the dead! Martha had sent Yesh a message while he was delirious with fever and dysentery, but he'd come too late. Apparently he'd stayed on another couple of days before he'd set out, by which time he, Lazarus, had died and had been buried in a rock tomb for four days. The next thing he knew, he heard a commanding voice and was stumbling out, wrapped up in linen. The bright light hurt his eyes and he felt really odd. Then Yesh gave him a hug, well, that was after he'd extracted himself from his sisters. Now they'd got him. What would they do? He hated to think.

★★★

The women slipped through the Sheep Gate and, with the

Temple grounds on their left, made their way to the entrance of the Antonia Fortress. No unusual activity there, so they circled round the Temple, wondering if that was where Yeshua had been taken. It might be where the Sanhedrin would meet, but surely not at this time. It was just after dawn. Again, nothing. So, puzzled, they set off south towards the upper city, planning to glean any news from John-Mark. Suddenly they could hear what sounded like an angry mob. They pressed themselves against the wall of the narrow street as around the corner came Roman soldiers. They were followed by Temple guards surrounding a man, and a noisy mob. Miriam saw with horror that the man was Yeshua. He had a broken nose, the blood matting his moustache and beard. His right eye was half shut in a badly swollen cheek and his lower lip was split. Strangely, he had a fancy purple cloak slung round his shoulders. Its meaning became apparent when the mob started chanting.

'Hail! King of the Jews. Behold your King! Hail! King of the Jews. Behold your King! Hail! King of the Jews ...'

Philetus had not deserted Yeshua, and was in the mob following him. He recognised the women and going over to them demanded, 'What are you doing here? It's not safe for you to be associated with him.'

'We had to come. Anyhow, what about you?' said Magda.

'I had to come too,' he acknowledged.

'What's happened to him? Where are they taking him?' she asked.

'It's totally irregular. They had a farce of a show trial at Caiaphas' house. He had summoned barely a quorum of the Sanhedrin. They couldn't get any of the accusations to stick as the witnesses kept contradicting themselves.'

'What are they accusing him of?'

'Oh, threatening to tear down the Temple and rebuild it in three days. Being inspired by Satan. Healing on the Sabbath.

Nothing except the last stuck, but then Caiaphas asked him, "Are you the Messiah, the Son of the living God?" Yesh looked him straight in the eye and said, "I am, and you will see the Son of Man seated at the right hand of God and coming on the clouds of heaven." Well that did it. Caiaphas and the others immediately cried, "Blasphemy!" and tore their clothes. They whipped up the crowd saying, "We don't need any other testimony. You have heard his blasphemy. What is your judgement?" "Death!" They called in unison. "Death." It was horrific, with the Sanhedrin behaving like a baying mob. Then they hit him, punching him in the face and spitting on him. One hit him on the back of the head and yelled, "Prophesy! Who hit you?"

'Then they took him to Pontius Pilate, and had him come out to them, so they wouldn't contaminate themselves by entering an imperial cult building before the Sabbath. He couldn't make head or tail of what they were asking. But, having found out that Yesh was a Galilean, he sent him to King Herod Antipas, as Galilee is in his jurisdiction. Herod asked him lots of questions but he refused to answer any of them. Herod sent him back to Pilate which is where we're going now.'

'Oh my poor, poor boy,' sobbed Miriam.

They followed the crowd back to the Antonia Fortress. The streets were filling up, as the Temple had brought in supporters. On their return, Pilate again came out in front of the Fortress. He looked pretty vexed. He had hoped Herod would have dealt with this problem, but it was clearly not going away. He felt completely out of his depth. He couldn't get his head around these Jews' idea of blasphemy and all their endless purity rules. All the food and other stuff they were so picky about, that they considered made them unclean. That would be a lifetime's study in which he had little interest. Now they had brought this man back, and wanted him dead, all for some bonkers outburst that he would destroy the Temple in three days and rebuild it.

Pilate sighed. Destroy the Temple and rebuild it in three days? What nonsense these Jews spouted! No one could take that claim seriously. This man Yeshua was obviously soft in the head.

However, he was uneasy for several reasons. Yeshua seemed far from being a simpleton or a crackpot. On the contrary, there was an unnerving depth and wisdom in his gaze, as if he could see deep into your soul; as if there was no hiding the truth from him. Whatever 'truth' was. He realised the priests had another agenda, but it was opaque to him. Jerusalem was a tinderbox at that moment, with thousands crowding in for Passover, including various zealot groups bent on insurrection. He couldn't allow this situation to get out of hand.

Caiaphas bowed. 'King Herod has returned him to you, Procurator. He has insufficient authority to condemn him to death. This man, Yeshua Bar-Joseph, has claimed to be "The Lord, The Almighty" and also to be the "King of the Jews". That is a direct threat against the rule of his Imperial Majesty Tiberius Caesar and against the Roman state.'

Now that was a charge that Pilate could comprehend. He turned to Yeshua.

'Are you the "King of the Jews?"'

Before Yeshua could reply there was a commotion behind Pilate and a flustered-looking servant whispered in his ear.

Pilate winced. 'What! Now? What does she want?' More whispering. Pilate held up his hand to halt the proceedings, indicating he would return soon, and turned into the gateway. He was just out of sight, but audible.

'Dearest I'm really busy. Can't this wait?' A woman's voice was heard murmuring. 'It was only a bad dream, woman, or have you become a prophet in your old age? I have to deal with him now!'

Pilate reappeared, looking flushed. Turning to Yeshua he repeated, 'Are you what they say you're claiming to be, the "King of the Jews"? Your own people and the priests have handed you over to me. What have you done?'

Yeshua replied, 'My kingdom is not of this world. If my kingdom were of this world, my followers would be fighting to keep me from being handed over to the Jewish authorities and to you. But as it is, my kingdom is not from here.'

'So you are a king?'

Yeshua responded, 'You say that I am a king. For this I was born, and for this I came into the world, to testify to the truth. Everyone who belongs to the truth listens to my voice.'

Pilate's heart sank. How could this man know that the concept of 'truth' was a major preoccupation of his? He heard himself say, 'What is truth?' and felt that gaze burn through him. He turned to the assembled priests and the crowd. 'This man has not committed a capital offence. In fact I cannot find him guilty of any crime under Roman law. I propose to release him.'

At this Caiaphas spoke up. 'He is inciting people to rebel against the Romans. If you let him go, he will become dangerous to peace in Judea, as more people become deluded with his kingly claim. Then he will mount an insurrection.'

From what he had heard of Yeshua's teaching, Pilate didn't believe this for a moment. However, he knew that the priests were perfectly capable themselves of inciting a riot, and that must not be allowed to happen. He was not flavour of the month back in Rome. One more civil uprising and he would be called home in disgrace. He tried one last time.

'I am prepared to flog him; however, I then propose to offer him as the one prisoner I customarily release at Passover time.'

'No, Sir. With respect, we request that you to release Barabbas.'

'Barabbas! He's a notorious murderer and if you want someone convicted of fermenting uprising against the Romans, he is your man, not this Yeshua.'

In no time the priests had got the crowd chanting, 'Barabbas! Barabbas! Barabbas!' They were in an ugly mood. The Roman guards shifted uneasily and one went to get reinforcements.

Pilate held up his hand and the crowed quieted. 'Barabbas it is. So what do you want me to do with Yeshua Bar-Joseph?'

'CRUCIFY HIM! CRUCIFY HIM! CRUCIFY HIM! WE HAVE NO KING BUT CAESAR! CRUCIFY HIM!'

The streets rang with the noise. Miriam fainted. Magda and Philetus propped her up against a wall and protected her from being crushed. Martha and Mary-Beth clung to each other, tears streaming down their faces. Yeshua was led back into the Fortress. A squad of soldiers formed a guard across the entrance, but it was just possible to see in.

Yeshua was stripped naked and his wrists manacled to a ring fixed high on a stone column, visible through the gateway. A burly soldier approached him holding a whip. It had a wooden handle, roughly as long as his forearm, with three leather thongs hanging from its end. Attached to their free ends were small, barbell-shaped lead weights, designed to rip flesh from the body. At the first stroke Yeshua shuddered as three bloody stripes appeared across his back. Each time the whip cracked, the crowd 'Ooohd' and 'Aaahd'. Soon his back, buttocks and legs were a mass of bloody stripes, with muscles being visible in places and even the white of a rib. Yeshua grunted in agony at every stroke. The soldier was spattered in blood. Thirteen stokes. Thirty-nine ripped-raw wounds. Blood flowed, merging and pulsing down his back.

Then they untied him, dragged his clothes back on him and jammed a circlet made of briar thorns on his head, piercing the skin. They continued the mockery, knocking him about, spitting on him, and several of the soldiers went down on one knee jeering, 'Hail! King of the Jews. Hail! King of the Jews.'

Pilate came out again and said, 'Look, I am bringing him out to you to let you know that I find no case against him.' As Yeshua emerged, Pilate declared, 'Here is the man!'

When the priests saw him, they shouted, 'Crucify him! Crucify him!'

Pilate responded, 'Take him yourselves and crucify him; I find no case against him.'

They answered, 'We have a law, and according to that law he ought to die because he has claimed to be the Son of God.'

Now when Pilate heard this, he was even more afraid. He re-entered his headquarters with Yeshua and asked him, 'Where *are* you from?'

Yeshua stayed silent.

'Do you refuse to speak to me? Don't you know that I have power to release you, and the power to crucify you?'

Yeshua replied, 'You'd have no power over me unless it had been given to you from above; therefore he who handed me over to you is guilty of a greater sin.'

Pilate continued to try to release him, but the mob cried out, 'If you release this man, you are no friend of Caesar. Everyone who claims to be a king sets himself against Caesar.'

Finally Pilate brought Yeshua outside and sat on the judge's bench at a place called the Stone Pavement saying, 'Here is your king!'

'Kill him! Kill him!' they shrieked. 'Crucify him! We have no king but Caesar.'

At this Pilate had a basin of water brought and washed his

hands, saying, 'I am innocent of this man's blood. Let it be on your heads.'

'His blood be on us and on our children!' the crowd responded.

Then he handed Yeshua over to be crucified.

CHAPTER 8

Crucifixion – Friday morning

The soldiers loaded a wooden crossbeam on to Yeshua's shoulders. There were two other men due to be executed with him, similarly laden. Due to the volatility of the crowd, Pilate provided a larger than usual contingent of soldiers, led by a mounted Centurion, Quintus Agrippa. Pilate had written out a notice to be nailed over Yeshua's head, which said in Hebrew, Latin and Greek,

Yeshua of Nazareth, the King of the Jews.

Caiaphas had quibbled at this, insisting, 'Don't write "The King of the Jews" but, "This man *said* I am the King of the Jews."'

Pilate regarded him with complete disdain, retorting, 'What I have written, I have written.'

The troops marched out, the prisoners interspersed between them. The crowd were crushed against the walls as the soldiers cleared the way. Philetus and the four women merged with the mob following the crucifixion squad. None of them had been able to watch Yeshua being flogged and had stuffed their fingers in their ears. Magda had thought Miriam would faint again, but she managed to remain conscious. Philetus had slipped around a corner and thrown up.

Before they reached the city walls, Yeshua stumbled and fell, the heavy crossbeam trapping him on the ground. A soldier removed it but Yeshua was barely able to stand and when it was dumped back on his shoulders, he collapsed. Realising that this would delay them, Centurion Agrippa glanced around the crowd, his gaze falling upon a stocky man with a shock of red hair.

'Hey! You! Yes ginger, I mean *you*! Carry his beam for him. Don't argue, just do it!'

Soldiers hustled the man towards Yeshua. He lifted the beam off him and onto his own shoulders. As Yeshua struggled to his feet their eyes met. Recognition flashed between them. Simon, shouldering the beam, walked alongside Yeshua the rest of the way, out of the city gate and up to a knoll called Golgotha, the place of the skull.

Upright posts were already in place. There they stripped the men naked and, laying them down with their arms outstretched along the crossbeams, they hammered long iron nails through their wrists. Two soldiers mounted ladders placed on either side of the post with the crossbeam carried between them balanced on one shoulder each. It slotted into a notch cut some ten feet off the ground and was secured with a rope. One soldier pulled out Pilate's notice from his belt and nailed it over Yeshua's head. Having descended, he twisted and bent up each of Yeshua legs, hammering a nail through the ankles. The same was done with the others. Their labels read, 'Robber'. It was still only three hours after sunrise.

Yeshua looked down at the execution party, the various members of the Temple and the crowd. They started mocking him again, saying, 'Ha ha! You who would destroy the Temple and rebuild it in three days, save yourself, and come down from the cross!'

'You saved others; can't you save yourself?'

'Let the Messiah, the King of the Jews, come down from the cross, so that we can see and believe.'

'He trusted in God. Let Him deliver him if He delights in him.'

Yeshua responded, 'Father, forgive them. They don't know *what* they're doing.'

Even one of the robbers had a go at him. 'Save us you bastard! Save us! What's the matter with you? Or aren't you the Son of God like they all say?'

The other robber was horrified. 'Aren't you afraid of God? We're all going to die together. Let's face it, we've been caught stealing, but this bloke's done nothing wrong. Yeshua, remember me when you come into your kingdom.'

He replied, 'Today you'll be with me in Paradise.'

One of the perks of being in an execution squad was that you got to keep the condemned men's clothes and possessions. Well, they wouldn't need them again. To avoid arguments the soldiers gambled for each piece, winner getting first choice, and so on.

'Let's play *Tens*,' said one of the soldiers.

'I'm thirsty!' croaked Yeshua. Given his blood loss, dehydration was setting in early. 'I'm thirsty.'

A soldier laughed and, getting the sponge he used for wiping his bottom, he doused it in vinegar, spiked it on his spear, and held it up to Yeshua's face. Yeshua gagged. Then he saw his mother and the other women along with Philetus. They were sobbing and could barely stand, supporting each other.

He addressed them, 'Mama, Philetus is now your son. Philetus, take care of our mother.'

Philetus put a protective arm around Miriam and nodded his assent.

As noon approached storm clouds rolled across the sky. It became darker and darker and the horizon shrank. Birds stopped singing. The air was charged with static. Agrippa's horse snorted, stamped its feet and tossed its head. Its eyes were wild and its mouth flecked with foam. He struggled to control it. The low pressure made the bystanders' heads feel like they would explode, but the storm wouldn't break. There was now no sound except that of the crucified men labouring for breath. Every so often, to try an ease the agony in their arms and the tightness in their chests, they would push themselves up on the nails in their ankles. This compounded their pain rather than bringing relief. Hours dragged by. Yeshua felt he was drowning, with waves of panic surging through him as liquid pooled in his lungs. Mouthing Psalms, he gasped,

> *'My God, my God, why hast thou forsaken me?*
> *Why art thou so far from helping me,*
> *and from the words of my groaning?'*

Then he stiffened. Throwing his eyes up to heaven he cried out, 'It's finished! Father, into your hands I commit my spirit!'

He died.

Thunder crashed around them, lightning cracking though the sky. A huge bolt hit the Temple. The earth shook, fissures opened up.

Centurion Agrippa almost lost control of his panicked horse. A wave of comprehension flooded him. He gasped, 'Truly, this man was the Son of God!'

CHAPTER 9

Remorse and despair – Friday

The city rubbish tip in the Valley of Gehenna was a dreadful place. It stank of fetid food along with that sickly-sweet smell of rotting flesh. Mattresses and clothes too far gone ever to be recycled littered the place. It was swarming with flies and rats flourished. Peter made his way up the far side of the valley, having slipped through the Essene Gate at dawn. He passed a bloated, decaying donkey and the smoke from scattered fires stung his eyes. He wanted to retch.

How could he have deserted Yeshua at his arrest and then denied even knowing him, when his accent gave him away? He, who had so boldly told Yeshua that he would die with him rather than ever desert him. Yeshua knew him better than he knew himself. He'd forecast that Peter would deny him three times before the dawn's second cock crow, and that was just what had happened.

He thought back to the first time he'd met Yesh. He'd heard about him of course, but thought it was all a bit hyped up. Then Yesh came alongside his boat while he was mending his fishing nets and looked at him with those penetrating eyes. 'Follow me.' That's all he'd said. 'Follow me.' And he did, as did his brother Andrew.

Then there was that time when his mother-in-law was so ill. She hadn't been able to get out of bed for days. They were really worried about her. Yesh laid his hand on her forehead, prayed, and she recovered. Just like that! That helped a bit when he explained that he would be leaving the family fishing business to follow Yesh.

He thought back on an extraordinary occasion when Yesh took him and the Zebedee boys up a mountain to pray. Suddenly, Yesh's face shone with an ethereal light and his clothes became dazzling white. Two other men appeared, similarly illuminated, the lawgiver, Moses and the Prophet Elijah. They spoke of Yesh's imminent departure. He, Peter, was so sleepy, but was transfixed by what he saw. He felt he had to say something and stammered out, 'Lord it's great we're here. Let's build three houses, one for you, one for Moses and one for Elijah.' What can he have been thinking of? While he rambled on, a cloud descended. It was terrifying! From the cloud came a booming voice that said,

'This is my Son, my beloved; listen to him!'

Then Yesh was just standing there alone, looking normal.

Peter's mind drifted back to when they had come into the region of Caesarea Philippi. Yesh had asked, 'Who do people say I am?' His brother, Andrew, offered, 'Some say John the Baptist, some Elijah, and others, Jeremiah or one of the other prophets.'

Yesh insisted, 'But who do *you* say I am?' And suddenly he, Peter, got it. He hadn't been sure until that moment, but all at once he got it, and said, 'You're the Messiah, the Son of the living God.'

Yesh responded, 'Blessed are you, Simon Bar-Jonah, for my Heavenly Father has revealed this to you. I shall now call you *Peter*, and on this rock I'll build my Church. The gates of Hell shall never overcome it. And I'll give you the keys of the Kingdom of Heaven. In my name you'll have the authority to forgive people's sins or to retain them.'

Then he told us not to tell anyone, as otherwise the people would make him king and expect him to overthrow the Romans, which wasn't why he'd come. We were rather disappointed because that's what we'd hoped Yesh would do.

He could still hear Yesh saying, 'I shall now call you *Peter.*' Yesh was always giving people nicknames. Mind you, the Zebedee boys weren't too thrilled with 'Sons of Thunder'! But they were such show-offs.

The sight of a man approaching jerked him out of his reverie. With a start he recognised him.

'Judas!' Peter shouted down the hill. 'You bastard! How could you betray us like that? Sneaking off from dinner. Leading those Temple guards to where we always hang out in the Garden. Then going up and kissing him. They're going to kill him now, you know that don't you? What could have possessed you?'

Peter glared down at Judas, who was still toiling up the hill towards him. He looked wretched, absolutely stricken, with tears streaming down his face, making rivulets in the ash-dust. Peter was shocked, not realising he looked much the same. He still had his sword and thought he would kill Judas then and there. But his limbs felt leaden. He was drained of energy and so just stood and waited as Judas approached him.

'I know that now, but I didn't realise at the time,' said Judas. 'I thought they'd just keep him out of the way until Passover was finished and then let him go. That's what they said they'd do. They just couldn't risk another riot like the one in the Temple when he crashed about, overturning the money-changers' tables and releasing all the animals. It was chaos. You saw him, lashing about with that rope-end. He'd gone completely crazy. He was going to get us all put away. When officers from the Temple approached me they implied they would charge him with a public order offence, detain him for a while and then let him go.'

'Bit naïve of you wasn't it? You're always accusing *me* of that,' Peter responded. 'But then you never were quite "one of us".'

'Oh and didn't you make sure I knew it!' Judas snapped back bitterly. 'You were always going on about me being a toff from down south. What's wrong with Judea? It's a lot more sophisticated than Galilee. But Yeshua preferred you guys, felt more at home with you northern oiks. You're his best mate, Simon, whom he nicknamed Peter, "Rocky". Pretty flaky, if you ask me. You generally open your mouth just to change feet, when not stuffing food into it. And wine for that matter. Yet, *you* get to go up the mountain with Yeshua and the Zebedee boys, all buddy buddy. You have Yeshua stay in *your* house. You even get to walk on water – though that didn't go too well in your case. But I'm the one who organises everything. I didn't ask to be treasurer. It's a real pain having to keep account of the money, handing it out for food and lodgings as well as for lepers and beggars, the lot. Then you accuse me of pilfering.'

'Well there never seemed to quite the same amount of money for food and stuff as we thought we'd been given. We noticed it just too often,' said Peter.

Judas continued, oblivious, 'It's all been going wrong recently. When we started it was fantastic. That ringing message: "The Kingdom of God is at hand. Repent and believe the good news." His preaching was so uplifting. The healings and the deliverance from evil spirits. The crowds that would follow us everywhere. And Yeshua was so pure. He'd given up the family firm to live as a wandering rabbi. Any money he was given, he always gave some to the poor, well, we all did. And he created food from nowhere. It was amazing! But then look what happened. He allowed himself to be slavered over by that woman with the perfumed ointment. It could have been sold for a year's wages. What a waste! For his burial indeed. That's what he said. In the past he would have put it to good use, but now he's just becoming a cult figure. All that triumphal entry, donkey riding, palm-leaf waving extravaganza into Jerusalem, just as it was filling up for Passover. And what was he was going on about at dinner? Eating his body and drinking his blood whenever you share bread and wine? That's disgusting! We can't even consume the blood of animals, let alone that of a person! How weird is that? He's completely lost it! The mob's pathetic, but he plays up to it. I think he really does believe that he's the Messiah, but he's gone a funny way about it.'

'Of course he's the Messiah!' shouted Peter 'Do you still not get it?'

'Well he's not throwing out the Romans is he? Crashing about in the Temple! He'll get us all killed. The authorities won't put up with any more of that. The Sanhedrin are terrified the Romans will take over the day-to-day running of everything, including the Temple, so they'll lose all their power, influence and income. The Romans don't want another riot. One more and Pontius Pilate will be recalled in disgrace. Everybody knows that. Pilate's in a really weak position. I decided that shouldn't happen. The Sanhedrin approached me and I thought it would be a way of getting him out of circulation for a few days. Just until after Passover and the fuss had died down. Then we could all go home.'

'What did they pay you?' Peter demanded.

'I've given back the money – threw it on the Temple floor as they wouldn't take it from me,' Judas replied. 'It was never about the money. What's thirty pieces of silver? Barely enough to buy a field.' Mind you, he thought, the High Priest Caiaphas did imply it was just a down-payment. 'But I was *so* wrong. I've betrayed an innocent man and now they're going to kill him. Peter, I don't know what to do. Could he ever forgive me?'

Peter just looked at him. Both men, their shoulders slumped, their faces tear-streaked, were utterly desolate, yet separated by a gulf, each in his own world of misery. Peter looked down and shook his head. They had shared three years of being together as Yeshua's disciples, walking the length and breadth of Judea and Galilee, as well as going into Samaria and the Decapolis. Day in, day out, sharing in his teaching and healing. Yet now Peter could find nothing to say. Judas stumbled on up the hill towards some scrubby trees. Peter didn't turn to look. He doubted he would ever see him again.

Later that evening Peter slowly made his way back to the city, pausing by a stream to wash off the worst of the ash. The moon was rising, but seemed strangely tinged with red.

CHAPTER 10

Death and burial – Friday, late afternoon

Pilate had given orders that the bodies should be disposed of before the Sabbath to avoid possible civil disruption. In good time Quintus Agrippa ordered that the robbers' legs be broken to hasten their deaths. A soldier swung the hammer at a leg and it shattered with a sickening crack. The man screamed. He slumped to one side, almost all his weight hanging on one outstretched arm. The other legged smashed, he hung limply, his breathing increasingly harsh. The same with the second robber. Gradually their breathing became shallower and more rasping. Finally it ceased. Just to make sure he was also dead, the soldier then jabbed his spear into Yeshua's right side, half way up the ribcage. Blood and a clear liquid, which had drained into his lungs, leaked out.

Joseph of Arimathea, who had been standing some way off, turned and went straight to the Antonia Fortress to ask Pilate for permission to bury Yeshua. Having found out, rather to his surprise, that he was already dead, Pilate gave him leave. Joseph went home to collect a shroud which he had had woven especially for his own burial. It was of the finest quality linen, over twice the length of a man's height and considerably broader than shoulder width. Picking up a smaller cloth, he invited Shabaka to accompany him with a makeshift stretcher. He also sent a messenger to Nicodemus, who would have wanted to be there. There would be no time this evening to prepare Yeshua's body properly for burial, as they had to be back before the sunset start of the Sabbath. Joseph returned to Golgotha. Most of the onlookers had dispersed. The bodies of the two robbers were to be thrown into a common criminals' grave. Quintus Agrippa allowed Joseph to take Yeshua away.

They used a pair of the soldiers' pincers to prise the nails from Yeshua's ankles. Then Shabaka climbed a ladder, wrapped the small cloth around Yeshua's head, concealing his face, untied the rope and bodily lifted him and the crossbeam down to the ground. Miriam and Magda collapsed onto it, kissing the body and weeping. Removing the wrist nails, they laid him on the stretcher and Philetus covered him with his cloak. Nicodemus arrived. Slowly, sorrowfully, the little cortège made its way up towards the limestone quarry where Joseph's family graves were sited. His personal tomb had never yet been used, though there were shelves cut to take several bodies.

Joseph unfolded the shroud and placed half its length along a shelf. Shabaka and Philetus removed the head-cloth, gently lifted Yeshua's body and placed it on the shroud. Joseph then folded the shroud over him, its full length reaching beyond his feet.

All covered their heads and Joseph led them in the Kaddish, the prayer for the dead.

'May God's great name be exalted.
Sanctified is God's great name in the world which He created according
to His will! In the world which will be renewed and where He will
give life to the dead and raise them to eternal life and rebuild the city of
Jerusalem and complete His temple there and uproot foreign worship
from the earth and restore Heavenly worship to its position and may the
Holy One, blessed is He, reign in His sovereign splendour. May He
establish His kingdom and may His salvation blossom and His
anointed be near. During your lifetime and during your days and
during the lifetimes of all the House of Israel, speedily and very soon!
And say, Amen.'

'Amen,' they chorused.

'May His great name be blessed for ever, and to all eternity! Blessed and praised, glorified and exalted, extolled and honoured, adored and lauded be the name of the Holy One, blessed be He, above and beyond all the blessings, hymns, praises and consolations that are uttered in the world! And say, Amen.'

'Amen'

'May the prayers and supplications of all Israel be accepted by their Father who is in Heaven; And say, Amen.'

'Amen'

CHAPTER 11

Desolation – Saturday

No one had slept. Some had dozed fitfully on couches and chairs. The men had congregated in the upper room of John-Mark's family home, where they had dined the night of Yeshua's arrest. Over the course of Friday night, various disciples had crept back there, hoping not to draw too much attention to themselves, but needing each other's company. Near midnight even Peter appeared, utterly desolate. His brother Andrew hugged him and they sat together in shock. At dawn a cock crowed, and Peter was once again engulfed in sobs. How could he have done it? How could he have denied knowing Yeshua? He, who had boasted that he'd die for him? He was inconsolable.

Breakfast had been left out in covered dishes before the start of the Sabbath, comprising bread, honey, dried apricots, figs, nuts and raisins. The whole house was in mourning.

Philetus said, 'I can't stop thinking about that extraordinary moment when Yeshua washed our feet before supper. The servant was horrified, did you see? That the Messiah, the Son of the living God, should wash our feet!'

'Are you still sure he's the Messiah?' asked Thomas. 'He's dead. It's over.'

'He's dead, but it's not over,' said Philetus. 'Remember when we were on our way to Jerusalem, he told us that "The Son of Man" - he often referred to himself that way - The Son of Man will be handed over to the priests and the scribes, and they'll condemn him to death; then they'll hand him over to the Gentiles; they'll mock him, and spit on him, flog him, and kill him. On the third day he'll rise again. Well, all the rest has happened. We have to believe he'll rise again.'

The others looked at him incredulously.

'Like he raised Lazarus after four days in his tomb?' asked Thomas.

'I'm not sure it will be quite like that. I don't know what to expect, but we have to believe. He told us to care for each other, to serve each other. Let's do that and see what happens. He entrusted Miriam into my care. His brother, James, remains sceptical, so I am to be a son to her.'

John-Mark and his father, Mark, entered the room. The others stood respectfully.

'I can't get out of my mind what Yeshua said and did at the end of the meal,' said John-Mark. 'I just don't understand it. He took a loaf of bread, blessed it, broke it, and gave it to us saying, "Take, eat; this is my body." Then he took a cup of wine, gave thanks to the Lord and told all of us to drink it with the words, "This is my blood of the new covenant, which is poured out for many for the forgiveness of sins. Truly I tell you, I'll never drink wine again until I drink it in the Kingdom of God." I just don't get it.'

'Nor do I,' said Philetus, 'but I think we should do it, because he told us to, and maybe as we do it, its meaning will become clear.'

Andrew urged, 'I'm sure he was the Messiah. No one other than the Lord could master the sea as he did. I saw him walking across the waves to join us in the boat. I couldn't have imagined it. It happened. We'd left him on the shore. We were well away from land, and he joined us.'

'Yes, yes, I remember, and I walked out to meet him, which worked fine until I thought about it. Then I sank,' interjected Peter. 'Also, he conjured up shoals of fish where there weren't any. I've been a fisherman all my life. If I haven't caught anything overnight, it's because there isn't anything there to catch. He was a carpenter for heaven's sake, what did he know about fishing? Yet he told me to put out my net on the other side of the boat and it nearly broke, there were so many fish.

'And the storm! Do you remember the storm, when we thought the boat would sink? There he was, asleep on a pillow. When I woke him, he talked to the wind and waves as if they were a couple of naughty boys. Immediately there was calm, with just a gentle breeze to get us to the shore.'

'Yes but he's dead!' half shouted Thomas. 'What can we do now?

'We wait and we pray,' said Philetus. 'It's the Sabbath. It's all we can do.'

Philip, one of the disciples who had remained silent until then, spoke up. 'He must be the Messiah. Only the Lord can do what he did. Apart from controlling the weather and commanding the waves, do you remember that last Passover time when he'd attracted five thousand families to listen to him? He asked me how we could buy food for all these people, as it was getting late. It was ludicrous! It would have cost eight months' wages. Then you, Andrew, turned up with that lad whose mother had thought to send him off with a packed supper: five buns and a couple of fish. Like that was going to help. Yesh got them all sitting down, prayed, giving thanks to his Heavenly Father, and got us to distribute the food. It just kept on coming, remember?' The others nodded. 'Everyone had enough to eat and there were twelve baskets of leftovers! Not even Moses could do that. When God fed the Israelites during the Exodus from Egypt they only ever had sufficient for the day. They had to trust that the next day God would provide again, but Yesh produced masses more than was needed.'

'Like the wine during that wedding at Cana,' interjected

Peter. 'We'd drunk the place dry and, to avoid the bridegroom being embarrassed, Yesh turned gallons of water into the finest wine, better than I'd ever drunk before. More than we'd already got through.'

'The Law was given through Moses, grace and truth came from Yeshua Messiah,' said Philetus. 'The Law should be sufficient for us to lead holy lives, only we never quite manage. The food and water that the Israelites were given was sufficient. But grace: undeserved, exuberant generosity. Yeshua offered us that grace from the moment he arrived. We have to believe it's not over.'

Silence fell. Time crawled by. Then Matthew started to reminisce. 'I remember the first time I saw him. I was at my tax booth. Yesh stopped by me and looked deep into my eyes, as if he could see into my soul. He said, "Matthew, you are a great worrier but you're putting your faith in fragile things. After all, you can't add a single day to your lifespan by worrying – rather the reverse! I know you have a well-paid job, and you feel you need it, in order to keep your family in comfort. But it must be hard having your fellow Jews despise you for collecting taxes for our Roman occupiers. Matthew, Matthew, stop worrying about where you'll live and what your family will eat and wear. The Romans strive for material possessions, but it doesn't make them happy. Your Heavenly Father knows what you need to live well. Look how he provides for wild animals and birds. They don't do a day's work, but are cared for. Don't you think you're much more important to God than them? Look how lovely flowers are. I tell you not even King Solomon in all his glory had finer robes. So don't worry about tomorrow. Tomorrow can take care of itself. Today's troubles are enough for today. Matthew, don't put you faith in perishable things, but build up your treasure in Heaven, by loving God and loving your neighbour as yourself. For where your treasure is, there will your heart be also. Strive first for the Kingdom of God and His righteousness, and you'll find that you're given all you need. Follow me."

'I didn't hesitate. I shut up my booth and invited him and you lot to come home with me. Then I sent out to my fellow tax collectors and invited them to dinner with us. I thought they all had to hear him. I remember him saying, "No one can serve two masters; for you'll either hate the first one and love the second, or be devoted to the second and despise the first. You can't serve God and money."

'Later on I heard that the Pharisees were shocked that this rabbi was sitting eating with us, semi-traitors, and other social undesirables! He confronted them with, "Those who are well don't need a doctor, but those who are ill. Go and learn what God meant when he said, 'I desire mercy, not sacrifice'. For I have come to call sinners, not the righteous." The irony was that the Pharisees all thought that *they* were righteous, because they kept all our exhaustive purity and behaviour laws. They were livid when he pointed out the hypocrisy of their behaviour, fulfilling the letter of the Law with respect to giving to charity, but ignoring its spirit. Once they'd donated their ten per cent of income to the Temple, they felt no further obligation to any beggar on their doorstep.'

He lapsed into silence. The hours dragged by. Occasionally one of them would go downstairs and stride around the colonnade, just to release the tension. Apart from breakfast, the upstairs pantry, next to the dining room, had bread, cheese, olives, dates, wine and water available to anyone who wanted it. This was so no one in the household had to work on the Sabbath. The pantry was linked to the ground floor kitchen by a staircase and a clever lift and pulley system, so the servants didn't have to carry everything up and down the stairs.

In the afternoon, Joseph of Arimathea arrived. His house

was nearby and of much the same design as Mark's. He had some startling news.

'The Temple's been struck by lightning and suffered a minor earthquake. There are blocks of stone lying around and the Holy of Holies was hit. The curtain separating it from the outer chamber was ripped right down the middle. You can still smell burning. No one can clear it up until after the Sabbath.'

Philetus said, 'Remember, we saw a flash and felt a tremor exactly the moment Yeshua cried out and died.'

'There's more,' said Joseph. 'The Temple authorities are so scared that we would tamper with the tomb, steal Yeshua's body and claim he had risen from the dead, as he said he would, that this morning they went to Pilate asking for a guard.'

'On the Sabbath!' expostulated Andrew.

'Pilate gave them permission but wouldn't send Roman soldiers, saying they should use their own troops. And that they could seal the tomb if they wanted to. I haven't been out there, but I gather a contingent of Temple guards left carrying lead, a fire pot and some other kit. I know the women want to prepare his body properly tomorrow but they won't be allowed to.

'The atmosphere in town is really jittery. It's as if people sense something really significant has happened, or is about to happen, but they don't know what. More Roman soldiers than usual are patrolling the streets and they are even more peremptory than usual. I was stopped twice and asked my business just on the way between our houses.'

CHAPTER 12

De profundis – Saturday

Downstairs in the parlour the women were also consumed by grief and shock. John-Mark's mother had tried to make them comfortable. Miriam and Magda had been offered one guest room and the sisters the other, but they had preferred to stay together. None of them could believe what they had seen with their own eyes.

'And a sword shall pierce through your own soul too. And a sword shall pierce through your own soul too,' Miriam muttered over and over to herself, picking nervously at a bowl of raisins.

'Did you hear them?' said Martha. 'The priests and scribes mocking him with, "You saved others, can't you save yourself? If you're the King of Israel, come down from the cross, and we'll believe in you. He trusted in God; let Him deliver him now; after all, he claimed to be the Son of God." Even one of the robbers being crucified with him rubbished him. He brought our brother Lazarus back from the dead, but who can do that for him?'

'Nothing is impossible for God,' said Miriam suddenly. 'That's what the angel told me when he told me that I would conceive the Son of God before my marriage. I was a virgin and asked how I *could* be pregnant. He said, "Nothing is impossible for God." He was right. My elderly cousin Elizabeth gave birth to John, who, thirty years later, baptised people in the river Jordan when they had repented of their sins. This was to prepare them for Yeshua; for the coming of the Kingdom of

God. The angel told me to call him Yeshua, meaning saviour, as deliverance comes from the Lord. Even Yeshua got baptised by John, though John said that it was all the wrong way round. That was the moment when John fully appreciated who Yesh was, not just his cousin, but the "Lamb of God" who would take away the sins of the world. I know Yesh's death has got something to do with that, but I don't know how and I can't bear it.'

She started to cry again and Magda wrapped her in her arms. She said, 'Miriam, tell us again the story of the angel and Yesh's birth. It's so inspiring and I find it comforting.'

Miriam recovered herself and continued. 'It was awful. First Jo was going to break off our engagement because he assumed I'd been unfaithful. Then the Lord sent him a dream and he came round, but the rest of the family didn't. I was an outcast. After that, we had to go down to Bethlehem to register for taxes, just before Yesh was due. The donkey ride was agony. Even worse, none of the family would travel with us and we couldn't stay with anyone in Bethlehem, as news of my disgrace had reached them. Yesh got born in the stable of the cheapest inn. They didn't have a reputation to lose.

'Shortly afterwards some shepherds came into town. You could hear people bolting their doors as soon as they saw them. But they came straight to the stable and fell down and worshipped little Yesh, saying that an angel had appeared to them, radiating light. He'd said, "Do not be afraid; I am bringing you wonderful news for the whole world. Today, your Saviour is born in Bethlehem, city of David. He is the Messiah, the Lord. You will find him all wrapped up and lying in a manger." Suddenly they were surrounded by angels singing, "Glory to God in the highest Heaven, and peace on earth among his favoured people." The shepherds left several lambs, which pleased the innkeeper no end.

'That wasn't all. Several days later, three extraordinary looking Magi from the East with their entourages arrived. They wore gorgeous robes, rode camels and were very exotic. Well, that caused a stir. The innkeeper didn't know what to do with himself. Suddenly his place was the star attraction. I was still pretty weak from the birth. They could barely fit into the stable. Apparently they'd gone to Herod to ask where the "King of the Jews" was to be born, as they'd interpreted star-signs that such a birth was imminent and had travelled a long distance to worship him. Well, as you can imagine, that put the cat among the pigeons in Herod's palace. He considered himself to be "King of the Jews". Moreover, he was setting up a rather fine dynasty. He sent them off to Bethlehem as that's from where the prophet Micah foretold Israel's ruler would come. He'd hoped they'd reveal our exact location, but in a dream they were warned not to return to Herod, so they bypassed Jerusalem overnight and slipped away. They brought Yesh the most amazing gifts. A jewel-studied casket filled with gold coins, a gold incense-burner containing the finest frankincense and, chillingly, a finely inlaid box containing myrrh - embalming paste. I still have it. We can use it tomorrow when we prepare his body properly.

'Eventually we took him up to the Temple to present him to the Lord. A night or two later, Jo had a dream that Herod was out to kill Yesh so we must flee. We escaped to Egypt, and the gold kept us going 'til he could get work. After Herod the Great's death we returned, by which time the family in Nazareth had accepted us back. King Herod Antipas seems no better than his father, murdering John when he pointed out his dubious lifestyle.'

'Yeshua saved my life,' said Magda. 'I was an outcast because I was possessed by demons. One day when I was fourteen, we'd run out of water and my mother sent me to the village well at midday. Well no one we knew was about, as it was far too hot, but there were some shepherds watering their flocks. I was frightened, but thought my mother would be cross if I didn't come back with water, so I carried on. First they started teasing me but soon they were pawing me. I tried to run but they caught me; then each of them raped me. They were laughing and saying that this was their "lucky well". Eventually they let me go. I staggered home but couldn't tell anyone what had happened. I was so ashamed. It would have brought dishonour on all my family. My sisters could never have married. I hid in bed for three days and then the voices in my head started.

You're dirty. You're evil. You're a curse on your family. This is all your fault. You led them on. You're a bad girl and a disgrace.

'Then I saw them, always just out of the corner of my eye. They looked like cockroaches. Sometimes I could feel them crawling over my skin, especially in bed, and I'd scream and thrash around, trying to get them off me. People told me I was imagining things, but they were real to me. The village found out, and I could hear people whispering about me behind my back. They could read my thoughts, they wanted to kill me, I wasn't safe anywhere. I was terrified. Sometimes I'd turn and argue with them and they would deny they had said anything, but just look at me as if I was mad. Eventually they drove me out of Magdala. They said I was possessed by demons. That I would bewitch the town, poison the well and make the flocks infertile. I went up to Jerusalem and had to go on the game. There was nothing else I could do or I'd have starved. I rented a squalid little room near the market and picked up clients in the street, taking them back there. Sometimes they were really rough and I got beaten up. One bloke tried to pimp me, add me to his brothel, take my money in return for "protection", but then he realised I was possessed and dropped me.

'One day Yeshua passed by, and I propositioned him. He turned and looked at me with such compassion. That had never happened before.

'"What do you charge?" he asked. I did a quick check of his clothes and thought it best not to ask too much.

'"A piece of silver," I replied.

'"I'll pay you that," he said, "but come and have a drink first." He led me to a bar, sat down and ordered us a flagon of wine. Then he looked deep into my eyes. It was as if he could see my soul. He asked, "How did a beautiful woman like you end up as a prostitute?" I found myself telling him the whole story. I'd never told *anyone* before. It was as if he had all day and no one else in the world but me mattered. When I'd finished, I was weeping. I felt so ashamed and all I was getting from him was love from those amazing eyes. He put his hand on my arm and said, "Mary from Magdala, you have suffered far more than you should. Be re-clothed in your rightful mind. I banish the demon voices, I banish the demon creatures and I banish the demon paranoia. Be gone! Never return! Mary, may you be restored to lead a pure life, to reverently praise your God. All your sins are forgiven. From now on I shall call you Magda. Follow me."

'And I was healed from that moment. I have served him ever since, rather than servicing him. He even offered me the silver piece, which of course I refused! Thinking back on it I could see how he got his dodgy reputation for hanging around bars with prostitutes. Lots of people must have seen us there, but he didn't mind.'

They were silent for a while, each woman lost in her own thoughts. Then Mary-Beth spoke up.

'I remember Yesh comparing himself to the suffering

servant in Isaiah. Think about it. If we take Isaiah Chapter 53, line by line, it could be all about Yeshua. More than once he suggested that to me. What's amazing is that it was written some seven hundred years ago!

'To whom is the arm of the Lord revealed? For he shall grow up before him as a tender plant, and as a root out of a dry ground: he hath no form nor comeliness; and when we shall see him, there is no beauty that we should desire him.

'He emerged from Nazareth. No one thought anyone significant could come from there. And you couldn't exactly describe him as good-looking. Yesh looked really ordinary, except for his eyes, which seemed to see straight through to your soul.

'He is despised and rejected of men; a man of sorrows, and acquainted with grief: … Surely he hath borne our griefs, and carried our sorrows: yet we did esteem him stricken, smitten of God, and afflicted.

'Look at the way he was mocked, hit and spat at on Friday. "You trusted in God, so let God deliver you, if you're the son of God, come down from the cross, if you're the King of the Jews. How are you going to destroy the Temple and rebuild it now?"

'But he was wounded for our transgressions, he was bruised for our iniquities: … and with his stripes we are healed. All we like sheep have gone astray; we have turned every one to his own way; and the Lord hath laid on him the iniquity of us all.

'He said that he had to suffer and die as a representative for all of us and our sinfulness. He, Son of God, God himself, had to take the burden of our sins as we could never live holy lives. Adam and Eve had shown us that. By suffering and dying, he would redeem us, like a slave being bought his freedom. His blood would cleanse us for ever, as the blood of a Passover lamb purifies us for the coming year. We would never again have to sacrifice animals to the Lord to wash away our sins. It has all been done by the Lord himself, through himself, to himself.

'He was oppressed, and he was afflicted, yet he opened not his mouth:
he is brought as a lamb to the slaughter, … He was taken from prison
and from judgement: … For he was cut off out of the land of the living:
for the transgression of my people was he stricken.

'Philetus said he didn't respond to any of the accusations against him. He only assented that he was the "Son of the living God", at which point Caiaphas screamed, "Blasphemy!" He also didn't respond to Herod or to Pilate. It was a completely sham trial. He had no justice.

'And he made his grave with the wicked, and with the rich in his
death; because he had done no violence, neither was any deceit
in his mouth.

'He died with those robbers either side of him, but we've buried him in Joseph's tomb, wrapped in his own linen shroud, one of the richest men in Jerusalem.

'Yet it pleased the Lord to bruise him; … when thou shalt make his
soul an offering for sin … by his knowledge shall my righteous servant
justify many; for he shall bear their iniquities.

'He said that by his suffering, both in body and soul, we should all be justified, be deemed righteous by God. Our wrongdoing washed away, as if it had never been. This so that God would be true to himself, exercising justice while offering mercy. Eventually we will live with him for ever. Yesh would lose everything, in order to give us everything. Only he, God, the creator of the universe, could do that. It is as if he is the *Word of God*, speaking salvation into being. The same *Word* that spoke creation into being.

'Therefore will I divide him a portion with the great ... because he hath poured out his soul unto death ... and he bore the sin of many, and made intercession for the transgressors.

'Made intercession for the transgressors. Do you remember he said from the cross, "Father, forgive them, they don't know what they're doing"? He also told the robber who appealed to him and acknowledged him as his Lord that he would be with him that day in Paradise. We have to believe that it is not all over, though I don't understand how.'

They sat in stunned silence looking at Mary-Beth incredulously.

Finally, Martha asked, 'When did he tell you all this?'

'Those times when you were getting the supper on, sorting out the house and being thoroughly annoyed with me sitting at Yesh's feet, listening to him, instead of helping you,' Mary-Beth replied.

'You did indeed choose the better role, though I can only imagine what the men would have said if there'd been no supper!' Martha responded.

Miriam said quietly, 'Now I realise that he was hinting at those things to me on several occasions, but I didn't want to hear them as I couldn't bear the thought of him suffering so. I'm sorry you don't think he was good-looking, as everyone told me he looked very much like me!'

'Perhaps he would have made a good-looking girl?' said Magda. 'Though his beard might have been a bit of a problem.'

They all smiled for the first time in days.

'He liked and valued women in a most unusual way,' she continued. 'I was with him when we were walking through such a crush. So many people wanted a piece of him and Jairus, the leader of the synagogue, came up, absolutely desperate. His only child was dying, his twelve-year-old daughter. He fell at Yesh's feet begging him to come at once. Yesh set off and then in the midst of the crowd he stopped and said, "Someone touched me."

'It was ridiculous. I remember Peter saying, "Lots of people must have touched you, hard to avoid with this crowd."

'"No," he said, "someone touched me for a purpose, I felt power flowing from me." No one moved, except Jairus, who was almost hopping up and down with frustration at the delay. Yeshua waited and finally this wretched woman crept out from the crowd and collapsed on her knees at his feet, in tears.

'"I have been so ill," she said. "I have been bleeding for twelve years and the doctors haven't healed me, but bankrupted me. I thought if only I could touch even your cloak, you would heal me. And you have. I can feel that I'm well. Forgive me."

'Yesh looked at her with such love. He said, "Be encouraged my daughter! Your faith has healed you. Go in peace."

Magda continued, 'I thought Jairus was going to have a fit. Here he was, an important man, being made to wait while this nobody was healed. Actually he did know her. It had been his job to keep her out of the synagogue all those years, because her menstrual bleeding made her unclean and she would have contaminated the worshippers. At that moment a servant came up and told Jairus it was too late, his daughter was dead. Yesh immediately said to him, "Don't be frightened, only believe and she'll be well." We arrived and already the wailing had

113

started. Yesh hushed the crowd, and announced that the girl was sleeping, not dead. They laughed at him. They'd seen dead bodies before, and knew the difference. He kept us all out except the girl's parents, Peter, and the two Zebedee boys. I'm not sure exactly what happened inside, but the next thing I saw was that the girl emerged, looking pale, but definitely alive, and eating bread and honey.'

***

As sunset approached it was decided that those still at Mark's house should stay there overnight. There were enough couches for the men and several spare bedchambers, so everyone could at least lie down in some comfort. Joseph had returned to his home. The women were invited up to the dining room to share evening worship. Apart from the set prayers, Philetus led them in Psalm 130:

'Out of the depths have I cried unto thee, O Lord.
Lord, hear my voice: let thine ears be attentive to the voice
of my supplications.
If thou, Lord, shouldest mark iniquities, O Lord, who shall stand?
But there is forgiveness with thee, that thou mayest be feared.
I wait for the Lord, my soul doth wait, and in his word do I hope.
My soul waiteth for the Lord more than they that watch for the
morning: I say, more than they that watch for the morning. Let Israel
hope in the Lord: for with the Lord there is mercy, and with him is
plenteous redemption.
And he shall redeem Israel from all his iniquities.'

CHAPTER 13

Harrowing of Hell – Saturday

Nel mezzo del cammin di nostra vita, me ritrovai per una selva oscura
chè la diretta via era smarrita.
Entering midlife, I found myself as if in a dark wood where the path
had disappeared.
Dante Alighieri, *Inferno, Canto* 1:1

Yeshua stood at a giant gateway with solid iron gates bolted shut. Carved in stone across the curved lintel was the phrase,
Abandon hope all ye who enter here.

No, he thought, they no longer have to abandon hope. I am their hope.

He picked up a stone and struck the gate three times.

'Open up in the name of the Most High God!'

He was no longer in pain. Glancing down he saw that the nail holes in his wrists and through his ankles were healed, but still rawly visible. His forehead felt tight and his nose was tender. He moved stiffly and felt somewhat detached from his body. He was wearing a long white robe, and his hair and beard were almost translucent. His eyes, however, burned like flame the minute he saw Satan framed in the gateway. Satan appeared as a tall, well-built man with wavy, blond hair. He had once been so handsome, with high cheekbones, a broad forehead, square jaw, pale skin and ice-blue eyes, but now his features were permanently twisted into a sneer of pride, envy and disappointment. He wore a long, black robe.

'We meet again Satan, or should I call you Lucifer, you

fallen angel? I have come to claim as many as you have in here who will believe in me.'

Lucifer sneered. 'You're my only failure, Yeshua. I did my best. Who else would have refused to use his miraculous powers to create food when he had been starving for forty days? Who else could have resisted testing the Lord's protection against an untimely death? Who else, indeed, would have turned down control of the world's entire population and its riches for eternity, just because he had a few scruples about whom he worshiped?

'And later, that Mary Magdalene, she was a real stunner. She worshipped the ground you walked on. You wanted her, I know you did, but you never even allowed yourself to fantasise about her, let alone touch her. Then there was that woman at Jacob's well. Five husbands! Half the rest of the village wanted a go. You never touched her either. As for that snivelling hussy who anointed you with perfume! You can handle eroticism like no other man. Had a soft spot for Rachel too I recall. She would have made you a nice wife. Oh, I was impressed! Irritated, but impressed. When they wanted to crown you king, you just slipped into the crowd. When the Pharisees accused you of worshiping *me*, and using *my* powers to do miracles, anyone one else would have blasted them off the face of the earth. You just quoted scripture at them. Even when you completely lost your cool, thrashing around in the Temple, throwing out the animal-sellers and overturning the money-changers' tables, you didn't actually hurt any innocent bystanders. No collateral damage. Just cleared out the courtyard, so the Gentiles could worship God, YHWH. Yes, *God*. I can say his name without fear, unlike your fellow Jews.

'Almost got you in that Garden of Gethsemane though. Bit of a wobble there, "Father, take this cup from me." Just recovered yourself in time. "Not what I want but what you want." How you stood that flogging and crucifixion without calling on a legion of angels to rescue you I'll never know. Your whole body was one screaming sea of pain and you felt completely abandoned. I know you did, I could feel it in you and I fed it to you. You even thought God had left you. Well, you weren't left up there too long. Six hours? Some men take three days to die, gradually choking as their lungs fill up with fluid, while suffering a raging thirst and the nails tearing their flesh. Not as tough as some, are you?'

Yeshua stood and looked at Lucifer. Once he had been so beautiful; the handsomest of all the angels. Lucifer, the light-bearer, the morning star. The prophet Isaiah summed him up,

How you have fallen from heaven O morning star, son of the dawn!
You have been cast down to the earth, you who once laid low the
nations! You said in your heart I will ascend to heaven; I will raise my
throne above the stars of God; I will sit enthroned on …. the utmost
heights of the sacred mountain. I will ascend above the tops of the
clouds; I will make myself like the Most High. But you are brought
down to the grave, to the depths of the pit.

Lucifer had challenged the authority and supremacy of God and so was banished from heaven.

'I saw you fall, Lucifer, remember? I saw you fall like lightning from Heaven. You got your own back, tempting Adam and Eve to eat the fruit from the tree of the knowledge of good and evil, which God had forbidden them to touch. For this act of disobedience and God's realisation that they would then be likely to eat the fruit of the tree of life, of immortality, enabling them to become like the Father and like me, they were expelled from Paradise. I'll see them shortly, they have suffered enough.'

Now Lucifer stood ashen-faced, his once handsome features

twisted into a grimace of bitterness and envy. Oh, he was King of the Underworld, of Sheol, and Prince of the Earth. But this was his moment of truth. He knew, in the end, that he'd lost the war, though there were still many battles to fight and many souls to be sucked down into his clutches. Yeshua had beaten him by dying. He didn't understand how, but, deep within him, defeat iced his very marrow.

'Let me pass,' commanded Yeshua.

Lucifer stood aside.

A cavernous entrance hall, seemingly hewn out of the living rock, opened up. It was dark and a sense of total despair and desolation pervaded the air. Grief, abandonment, isolation, yet crushing proximity and horrific noise surrounded Yeshua. It was terrifying. He started to sweat. Three corridors led off the entrance hall. From the first one billowed sulphurous fumes and choking smoke. Yeshua's eyes smarted, streaming; then they extinguished the effect. He entered. The corridor opened up into an enormous cavern. He saw bodies writhing and screaming in pain. Molten lead was being poured into their mouths by laughing little devils. Red-hot branding irons were being pressed against men's flesh. Women were being mutilated. It was insufferable, and they could be here for eternity.

Not if I can help it, thought Yeshua. His heart ached with love for these wretched souls. How he longed to gather them all up as a hen would her chicks under her wings. But not all would be willing, some would remain desolate. He yearned to heal and protect them.

He walked to the centre of the cavern. As he did so, the fires dulled, the heat faded, the clashing din was silenced and the devils shrank away into the shadows. In the clearing air a cool breeze played around the tortured bodies. He had everyone's full attention.

'Come to me all of you who are burning and in pain. You,

who are consumed by pride, envy, anger, gluttony, lustfulness, material greed and even laziness. I am the living water which will restore you. Whoever drinks from me will never be thirsty again. Whoever is washed in me will never be dirty again. Whoever offers me to others will be forever blessed.'

'But who *are* you?' gasped a man, who was covered in sores and boils. Yeshua looked at him and smiled tenderly. He saw that the man wore a faded, tattered robe which had once been magnificent. On it he could just read the embroidered words, *My name is Ozymandias, King of Kings. Look on my works ye mighty and despair!* Around his neck was a chain on which hung a cartouche. Yeshua realised he had seen it somewhere before: a circle with a dot in its centre, a sceptre topped with a jackal's head, a seated goddess topped with a feather, an adze, a wavy line, and another dotted circle. The irony was not lost on Yeshua, of his offering the Egyptian Pharaoh, Ramesses II, a path to freedom, as had Moses all those centuries ago, when he led the Israelites out from Egyptian slavery to the Promised Land.

'I am the *Word of God*, I created everything from the beginning and nothing that has ever existed was formed without me. In me is life, and that life is the light of all people. I shine in the darkness and it cannot overwhelm me. Alas, many prefer darkness, because their deeds are evil. You, here, who believe in me now, to you I will give power to become children of God, born this time not of your parents, nor by some whim of fate, but of God. Believe in me and I shall take you to God the Father, who loves you. He, I and the Holy Spirit will bring you home. Come!'

'How do we know you're not just trying to trick us to an even worse place?' spat out a man.

Yeshua turned to him. He looked older than when they had last met.

119

'Oh my Gawd!' gasped Jac. 'I'm *so* sorry. I know we shouldn't have planned to sell you. We was short of funds see? Didn't know when we would get more work. Can you ever forgive me? You got your cloak back.'

'No thanks to you,' laughed Yeshua. 'Of course I forgive you Jac. Follow me.'

Gradually the tortured souls drew forward and each in their turn confessed their sins, how they had hurt and wronged others. They were absolved, blessed and moved out into the entrance hall. The devils remained gibbering in corners, unable to touch anyone. But not all came forward. Some grumbled or cursed. Some shouted that they didn't know why they were there and it was all everyone else's fault and they were damned if they were going to confess sins they hadn't committed just to please this bloke who thought he was God.

When all had come out who were going to come, Yeshua left them in the entrance hall and entered the second cave. An icy blast hit him, knocking the air from his lungs; he could barely breathe and the cold cut straight through him. The glare was so dazzling he had to squint. Lightning and thunder crashed around him. Hail stung his face.

His presence stilled the storm. As it subsided, he saw people bowed down with heavy weights, some wearing iron shackles, some with millstones round their necks, all labouring under loads too heavy to bear, while suffering frostbite and gangrene. His heart ached for them.

He said, 'Come to me all of you who are loaded down with guilt, with anxiety, shame, worry, regret, addictions and hopelessness. I will release you. Take my yoke upon you and learn from me; for I am humble and gentle of heart, and you'll find rest for your souls. My yoke is easy, my load is light.'

A woman's voice snarled, 'What's your "load" then? What d'you want from us?'

'Repent and hear the good news.'

'And if we say we're "sorry", what *good news* would that be then?' the voice retorted.

'You have to *be* sorry, not just *say* it. I am the *way* and the *truth* and the *life*. If you follow me, if you declare with you hearts and minds the truths of your life and that you are truly sorry for all the hurt you have caused others, all the damage you have done, and the things you should have done but didn't, all the needless suffering of which you have been part, then that truth will set you free. I'll give you a new life. I'll take you from this place of torment and bring you to a New Jerusalem. That city shines with God's glory, a jewel-like radiance, clear as crystal. It's surrounded by a high wall with twelve gates. Each gate is guarded by an angel and has one of the tribal names of Israel inscribed on it. However, the New Jerusalem is open to *all* who repent, to Jews and Gentiles, slaves and free, men and women, all who acknowledge me to be their Lord, along with the Father and the Holy Spirit.'

'Is that all? Just say sorry and follow you?'

'No,' replied Yeshua. 'It is to *be* sorry, not quite so easy, but try it; because you're worth it.'

A man emerged from the mist. He wore a battered crown and had swords sticking through him on which hung heavy weights tearing his flesh. His fingers and toes were lost to frostbite.

'I am Herod the Great. King of the Jews.'

'Was,' corrected Yeshua. 'You tried to have me killed when the Magi came to you asking where I was to be born. We escaped to Egypt until you were dead. However, you did slaughter all the baby boys in Bethlehem. That, along with all your other crimes. Will you repent of each and every one? I've got all day.'

Herod stared at him. He was in unutterable pain yet he

wasn't sure if he could humble himself before this man. Man? Was he a man? He appeared like a man, but no man had ever entered Hell like this. He diffused a golden light, he had a look of such compassion on his face, and he had stilled the storm. Yeshua turned away to address others present. They came to him singly and in groups; men, women and children, weeping, shaking and confessing their sins, begging for forgiveness and receiving Yeshua's blessing. They filed into the entrance cavern. When no more came forward, Yeshua left.

Finally, he turned to the last cave. Here an eerie silence reigned. It was pervaded with a sense of desolation, isolation, bereavement, grief too deep for words. A heavy weight where the heart should be. Every soul was utterly alone, locked in loneliness, longing for human contact of any kind. Even cruelty would be better than this emptiness. Hollow and vacant-eyed they looked at him, unable to see each other. His heart melted.

He declared, 'I am the A and the Z, the beginning and the end. I am the bread of life, the path to salvation, the living water. Those of you who conquer your pride and repent will inherit everything. I will be your God, and you will be my people.'

Although unable to perceive each other, a couple approached him with their adult son. He had a nasty mark burned into his forehead. He hung his head, he couldn't look at Yeshua. He spoke so quietly that he could barely get the words out.

'Yeshua Messiah, Son of God, have mercy on me, a sinner. Yeshua Messiah, Son of God, have mercy on me, a sinner. Yeshua Messiah, Son of God, have mercy on me, a sinner.'

Yeshua licked his thumb and stroked it across the man's forehead, erasing the brand.

'I killed my brother, Abel, because I was jealous. His sacrifice was acceptable to God, mine wasn't.'

'Do you know why one was and one wasn't, Cain?' Yeshua asked gently.

'Yes. He offered his finest lamb; my vegetables were a bit second-rate. I'd thought I'd keep the best for a bit longer. I'm sorry. Actually this place isn't much different from my life east of Eden. I always felt an inner emptiness, a separation from God, so I could never make real relationships with people. My wife and children suffered both for what I had done and who I had become.'

As he confessed he became able to see those around him. With a start he realised the identity of his companions.

'These are my parents, Adam and Eve!'

'Yes I know,' Yeshua replied, and turned to them. 'You had it all. Paradise was yours. You could eat almost everything that grew in the Garden; you could play with the animals; you could walk and talk with God in the cool of the day. Yet it wasn't enough for you. That one tiny little prohibition, it nagged at you didn't it? Day and night, "Why can't we eat the fruit of that tree? It looks gorgeous. What's the knowledge of good and evil anyway?" Lucifer, the serpent, beguiled you and you did eat. The tree of life would have been next. You wanted to know everything, to live forever, to become divine. Like Lucifer, which is why he's here. It was not to be. I know putting Archangel Michael at the entrance with a flaming sword was a bit melodramatic, but you had to realise, that was it! You could never return.'

They gazed at him beseechingly, not daring to hope. They had indeed abandoned hope on entering this terrible place. Yeshua smiled at them, almost wept, love overflowing his heart.

'You were the first man, Adam, I am the first and the last. I have come as a second Adam to rescue you and all who sin and fall short of the glory of God. Believe in me and I will take you to the Father.'

They fell to their knees, tears streaming down their cheeks, noses running, heaving sobs. Yeshua went forward, lifting them gently to their feet.

'You will live again in a new Heaven and a new earth,' he said, 'where again the home of God is among mortals. We will dwell with you, and you shall be our people. We shall wipe every tear from your eyes. Death will be no more; mourning, crying and pain will be no more, for the first things have passed away. See, I am making all things new. Everything's complete! I am the start and the finish. Come!'

Then another man emerged from the darkness, a raw-red weal around his neck. He hesitated, fearful of rejection. Could he ever be forgiven?

'Judas!' cried Yeshua. He rushed up to him, flung his arms around him and hugged him. 'Judas! When did you get here?'

'Not long before you. Peter's in a terrible state. Can't forgive himself for denying knowing you. He'd done a runner to the Valley of Gehenna, I met him there. I thought he'd kill me, but he didn't have the heart.'

'I'm delighted to hear it. He's a fine one that Peter, but impulsive. He is the rock on which I will build my Church. Him, and a man from Tarsus you haven't met, called Saul. He doesn't know it yet, but I'll engage with him when *his* time has come. So, what happened to you after I was taken to Caiaphas' house?'

'I realised I'd made the most terrible mistake. I thought they'd just arrest you and keep you out of the way until after Passover. Maybe beat you up a bit, then let you go.'

'Bit naïve of you wasn't it?'

'That's what Peter said. I realised almost immediately they were out to kill you or at least to get the Romans to do it, as they lacked the legal right of execution. The blasphemy charges are what did it with the crowd. I gather Pilate lost his nerve after being threatened with another riot. Mind you, they couldn't get your accusers to agree on anything, the whole trial was a bit of a shambles, apart from being irregular, so early in the day, with a handful of sleepy Sanhedrin. When you were taken to Pilate, I went back to the Temple and tried to get them to let you go. They just laughed at me. They wouldn't even take the money back, so I threw it on the floor. I heard what happened when Pilate condemned you. Then I left the city and met Peter. He looked terrible; eyes swollen and covered in ash. Oh! That place stinks. I left him, went up to the trees and hanged myself. "Cursed is he who is hung on a tree." Isn't that what scripture says?'

'You and me both,' smiled Yeshua.

'I'm so, *so* sorry. I was so stupid. Can you ever forgive me?' choked Judas.

'Of course I forgive you. However, I can't help the fact that throughout the future you're going to have a really rubbish reputation.'

Judas smiled through his tears; at least Yeshua hadn't lost his sense of humour. He left to join the others waiting to go. Others straggled after him, looking stunned and uncomprehending, but deeply relieved. Eventually Yeshua emerged and strode up to Lucifer who was still standing in the entrance. As he did so another man was being wrestled into the gateway by a bunch of devils. It was the robber who had cursed Yeshua on the cross, demanding that he save them all. He recognised Yeshua and shouted, 'What the hell are you doing here? Thought they said you was God. You died fast enough. They broke my legs. D'you know what that felt like after I'd been hanging for hours? Didn't think I could feel more pain. How wrong I was. What you doing here anyway?'

'Well I could take you out of here now if you will repent of your wrongdoing and acknowledge me as your Lord.'

'Why should I? Course I stole, but had no choice, did I? We had nothing. Dad left and Mum couldn't cope. Always drunk she was. Got the money from her fancy-men and drank it all. We was starving. Went to the Temple but they just talked pious and gave us nothing. Joined a gang. They was my real family. Felt I belonged for first time ever. Course I stole. Why wouldn't I? Rich got it coming to them. Snotty bastards. What you looking at? You can go to Hell you can! Could've saved us. Didn't. Well go to Hell, "King of the Jews"!'

Yeshua looked stricken as the robber was bundled through to the first cavern. He heard him scream. He turned away, faced Lucifer and commanded, 'You will let my people go.'

Lucifer gestured and two devils opened up the gates. The penitents streamed out, Yeshua leading the way. Lucifer looked on, hatred burning in his eyes. When all who were going had left, he shrugged and had the gates closed. No matter, there would soon be plenty more souls to replace those who had gone. His work on earth was far from done. He might have lost the war in the long term, but there was still a lot of fun to be had in the meantime.

CHAPTER 14

Consolation – Sunday

On Saturday night all had been made as comfortable as possible in Mark's substantial house, and all had slept from sheer exhaustion. Magda woke very early on Sunday morning. She tossed and turned and realised she would have to get up. She crept out of the bedchamber she had been sharing with Miriam, taking the bag of spices and herbs which the cook had given her for embalming Yeshua. Miriam would come with the others later, bringing the myrrh, but Magda couldn't wait. She let herself out onto the street, closing the door quietly, and hoping the doorman wouldn't worry that it now looked as if it had been left unbolted all night. It was still dark, but in this, the smartest residential street in the city, torches still flared in their wall-brackets. She walked north, past Herod's palace and out through the Joppa Gate, the guards sleepily letting her pass. It was very dark, the moon being low in the sky. She hadn't thought how she would see the way to the tomb, she just felt she had to be there. Stumbling occasionally, Magda made her way to the quarry, the limestone faintly reflecting such light as there was. She heard a distant tinkling of a goat bell, and hoped she wouldn't disturb a dog. Dawn was just starting to light the eastern sky. She successfully negotiated the stream and climbed up to the tomb.

Magda rounded the bend and froze. The stone had been rolled away! The stone with which Shabaka had closed the entrance, and which would have needed all four of the women to move, had been rolled aside. Magda crept up. She could hear two guards snoring loudly nearby, fit to wake the dead. As she approached the tomb entrance she peered in and saw a young man sitting opposite where Yeshua had been laid. He glowed with light. Yeshua's shroud lay flat on the slab. There was no trace of a body.

The man said to her, 'Don't be afraid. I know you're looking for Yeshua, who was crucified. He is not here.'

Magda turned and ran, not waiting to hear any more. She hurtled down the hill, splashed into the stream, recovered herself and fled all the way back to the city. The Roman guard looked a bit surprised to see her back so soon, and in such a state, but said nothing. He couldn't begin to understand these Jews and their weird religious beliefs and practices. So he just did his job.

Magda hammered on Mark's door and flew in the moment it was opened, not even acknowledging the doorman. She sprinted up the stairs and barged into the dining room where the men were in various stages of dress. As one, they looked horrified.

'Peter! Philetus! They've taken Yesh from the tomb, and I don't know where they've laid him!'

The two men leaped up, ran down the stairs, past the bemused doorman and up the street. They slowed down to exit the gate, so as not to draw attention to themselves. As soon as they were out of sight they broke into a run again. Peter was the more heavily built of the two and Philetus outstripped him, getting to the tomb first. There was no sign of the guards, or of anyone else. He bent down to look in and saw the shroud seemingly having collapsed flat in the absence of a body, with the folded head-cloth lying separately. Peter arrived, panting, and rushed straight past him, into the tomb. Philetus followed and, as he gazed at the shroud, belief seeped into him. Yesh had said that he would rise from the dead and this must be the explanation; however, he was still very puzzled. By this time Magda had joined them.

'You see! You didn't believe me, but you see! There was this young man all in white who seemed to glow. He started to talk to me but I didn't wait to hear what he had to say.'

'Well he's not here now and the guards have done a runner. That could be very embarrassing for someone,' Philetus responded. 'We should take the shroud back.' They carried it reverently outside. Peter took one end and Philetus the other and they opened it up in order to fold it neatly. As they held it full-length Magda said, 'Look!'

'Well of course there are bloodstains,' said Peter.

'No. Look more closely, angle it towards the light … and now away. Don't you see those marks?' There was the faintest of images of what might have been a body lying on its front and on its back head-to-head, seemingly sketched or perhaps scorched onto the linen. The closer she looked the less she could see, but standing back, there was clearly an extraordinary image.

'That definitely wasn't there when we wrapped him in it,' she said firmly.

'Maybe it will become clearer when we look at it later. Now I think we should go back to the others,' said Philetus.

The two men left, but Magda stood desolate and weeping. She bent over to look into the tomb. Her eyes widened as she saw two white-clothed angels sitting at each end of where Yeshua had lain. In unison they asked, 'Woman, why are you weeping?'

She replied, 'They've taken away my Lord, and I don't know where they've laid him.'

When she'd said this, she turned around and saw Yeshua standing there, but she failed to recognise him. He said, 'Woman, why are you weeping? Whom are you seeking?'

She responded, 'Sir, if you've removed him, please tell me where you've put him, and I'll take him away.'

Yeshua said, 'Magda!'

Wide-eyed, she shrieked, 'Teacher!', flinging herself into his arms. He was solid, as he always had been. Those carpenter's muscles hadn't atrophied during his ministry, as he often fixed broken furniture wherever he stayed, in order to help pay for his upkeep. He looked a bit different, but it was hard to say how. She sobbed on his shoulder and kissed his neck over and over again. Yeshua stroked her hair which was cascading down her back, all dishevelled.

When she had recovered herself sufficiently, Yeshua said, 'Don't hang onto me now, because I've not yet ascended to the Father. But go to my followers and tell them that I am ascending to my Father and your Father, to my God and your God.'

Mary Magdalene drifted back to Jerusalem in a daze. Had she imagined this? No, he was real. He was solid. She had seen the healed wounds in his wrists. He was the same, but different. Her heart leaped and she laughed out loud. She was so happy. She thought her chest would burst. She was crying and laughing all at the same time. As she neared the gate several people glanced at her, then quickly looked away. That was how they used to treat her when she was possessed, but she didn't care. She floated down the street and knocked at Mark's door. The doorman was thoroughly puzzled at the comings and goings, but his not to reason why. Everyone was out in the courtyard talking excitedly but silence fell as she entered, the sight of her was so arresting.

'I have seen Yeshua!' she exclaimed. 'I have seen Yeshua and held him and he's real and he's alive and it's all true and he has risen from the dead and everything he said would happen has happened!'

'Calm down my dear, and tell us exactly what you saw,' said Mark.

But Miriam rushed up to her. 'Tell me! Tell me! What did you see? Was it really him? Can you be sure?'

'He told me to tell you that, "I am ascending to my Father and your Father, to my God and your God."'

The women were in each other's arms. The men were standing around stunned. Could he really have appeared to a woman before showing himself to any of them? And then left her to tell them about it? It seemed most unlikely, but she was convinced, and Yeshua had been very fond of Magda. A hush fell over them and simultaneously each felt a tingling sensation throughout their bodies. Yeshua was standing in their midst. They hadn't seen him enter but he was definitely there, smiling broadly. He lifted his mother bodily off the ground and hugged her.

He said, 'Peace be with you all. Yes, it's definitely me. No more sword in your soul, Mama. Be happy. What the Angel Gabriel told you all those years ago is being fulfilled. I am the Son of the Most High, and the Lord God will give me the throne of our ancestor David. Just not in the way people have expected. I *shall* reign over a kingdom without end.'

He released her and then embraced everyone in turn. He showed them his healed wounds, including the spear thrust in his side.

At that moment Joseph of Arimathea, Ruth, Rachel and her husband, and Shabaka arrived, having been fetched by Thomas.

Yeshua turned to Joseph, hugged him and said, 'Joseph, your pride has been forgiven. You kept your promise. Deliverance belongs to the Lord.'

Joseph choked up and huskily whispered, 'My King and my God.'

Shabaka towered over Yeshua as he enveloped him in an embrace. He then removed his lion god amulet and laid it aside.

Yeshua turned to Martha, 'Now you can begin to understand what I told you when you came to meet me after Lazarus' burial. Remember? I said, "I am the resurrection and the life. Those who believe in me, even though they die, will live, and everyone who lives and believes in me will never die."'

He then announced, 'Ransomed, healed, restored, forgiven. Over time you will increase your understanding of what has happened here. All authority in Heaven and on earth has been given to me. Go therefore and make disciples of everyone, baptising them in the name of the Father and of Yeshua the Son and of the Holy Spirit, and teach them to obey everything that I have commanded you. Teach them to love the Lord their God with all their heart, with all their soul, with all their mind and with all their strength. Teach them to love their neighbours as themselves. And teach them who their neighbours are, and what that really means. Furthermore, remember, I am with you always, to the very end of time.'

Peter asked, 'Yesh, where have you been?'

'I have been freeing souls from Hell, at least those who wanted to be freed.'

'So who got out?'

'That's not for you to know Peter.' Yeshua looked around, 'Where's Thomas?'

'Oh, he stayed behind, having called us. He'll be back soon,' said Shabaka.

Then Yeshua was gone. Just as he had come. No one saw him leave, he just wasn't there any more.

Miriam burst into song.

'My soul magnifies the Lord,
and my spirit rejoices in God my Saviour,
for he has looked with favour on the lowliness of his servant.

Surely, from now on all generations will call me blessed;
for the Mighty One has done great things for me,
and holy is his name.
His mercy is for those who fear him
from generation to generation.
He has shown strength with his arm;
he has scattered the proud in the thoughts of their hearts.
He has brought down the powerful from their thrones,
and lifted up the lowly;
he has filled the hungry with good things,
and sent the rich away empty.
He has helped his servant Israel,
in remembrance of his mercy,
according to the promise he made to our ancestors,
to Abraham and to his descendants forever.'

At this point the cook came bustling back from the market, with a couple of servants doing the heavy lifting. 'I've just got a load of fresh eggs from the countryside, so I think you can all have scrambled eggs for breakfast,' she announced.

Suddenly they realised they were ravenously hungry, having not eaten much over the last forty-eight hours. Soon they could hear the sound of a pan sizzling in the kitchen and they crammed into the breakfast parlour, laughing and joking and not understanding what had happened but just being aware that it was brilliant. They couldn't get over it.

The cook was consulting Mark, who turned to the assembled company and said, 'Do please all come back for dinner this evening. Cook has found some excellent Roman rabbits and she will be making her famous rabbit stew. Martha, do please bring Lazarus. Joseph, bring your whole family; also Nicodemus. Today we truly have something to celebrate. Yeshua Messiah is risen!'

'He is risen indeed,' affirmed Magda.
Then all the others joined in.
'He is risen indeed.'

EPILOGUE

The end is in the beginning

Cyrene, some 15 years later

From Simon, master baker, in the city of Cyrene, along with my sons Alexander and Rufus, to Philetus of Galilee and Miriam, mother of Yeshua Messiah, residing in Ephesus. Greetings.

Janni Bar-Joseph brought us your letter on his way from Alexandria to Tripolis. I am so glad you are keeping in good health. I am sure Yeshua would be proud of his younger brother James becoming leader of the community in Jerusalem. I imagine that the earlier fraternal rift had grieved him, so better late than never. Janni was also able to give us news of other followers of the 'Way', as we now call ourselves. We have small communities scattered along the north coast of Africa who believe that Yeshua is the promised Messiah, and has come to save us from our sins.

As my health is deteriorating, I thought this would be a good time to record some of the events which have occurred since we met all those years ago. It was such a shock seeing Yeshua again, so beaten up and in such terrible circumstances. It seemed a lifetime from when we had last met in that Temple schoolroom. While I carried Yeshua's crossbar, my young sons, Alexander and Rufus, who were with me, lost themselves in the crowd as best they could, given their bright-red hair. We did not stay to watch him die, but returned to our lodging-house in a daze, and I told the boys about our first meeting. As a family we were still grieving the death of their mother in childbirth the year before. Alas, our baby daughter, Joanna, only survived her by a few days.

We had planned to stay in Jerusalem until Pentecost. As you remember, after Passover the place was in uproar. Firstly there was the damage to the Temple, interpreted by many as a bad omen. Then there were the rumours swirling around that Yeshua had been raised from the dead. Others said his body had been stolen, so his followers could claim his resurrection. There was also a conspiracy theory that the Romans had removed the body so that the tomb could not become a place of pilgrimage. In that case, all they would have had to do to quash the rumours that Yeshua had resurrected was to produce his remains. Yet others suggested that he had never really been dead and had revived in the cool of the tomb and escaped. That last idea was laughable. Roman soldiers don't make that sort of error.

We caught up with some of your colleagues, Peter and Andrew, who told us that they had seen Yeshua. Somehow it seemed more believable because he had first appeared to a woman who then told the men. No one would make that up. I still remember when we were with you on the Mount of Olives, and Yeshua appeared from nowhere. I knew he was real, we embraced and I introduced him to my sons. (How could you embrace a ghost?) He explained that, when he had claimed that if the Temple was destroyed he would rebuild it in three days, he was referring to his own body as the 'temple', the residing place of God. Many came to believe in him during that meeting. Then he blessed us and disappeared. We had the good fortune in the following days to spend time with Andrew and Philip, who recounted much of his ministry and teaching. When we were told that he had described himself as the 'bread of life', I had this really strange sensation that, as a baker, he was talking directly to me, and that I must pass on this 'bread' to others.

How he must have upset the religious rulers with his back-to-basics message of love, mercy and justice, rather than endless dressing-up, ritual and show. It reminded me of that highly charged encounter he had with Caiaphas when we were boys. Our most exciting lesson ever. Philip described one miracle after the next. Normally I wouldn't have believed such tales, but in the circumstances they were utterly convincing. Andrew emphasised that, as the prophets had foretold through the scriptures, in the arrival of Yeshua, the Kingdom of God had come very close, and that He would return in glory to restore the world to the way the Lord intended it to be, before Adam's fall from grace.

The love all his disciples showed not only to each other and to his followers, but to everyone they met, was tangible. We still remember with wonder when you, Philetus, baptised me and my sons in the name of the Father, Yeshua the Son and the Holy Spirit. We felt reborn, restored, healed, forgiven. Our lightness of being was beyond description. The closest I can get to it is when the lightest sponge melts on the tongue, suffusing the mouth with sweetness. Finally we were in the street at Pentecost when you were all preaching the good news of his resurrection to anyone who would listen. You appeared to have flames dancing over your heads and, as people came to believe, those flames divided and leaped onto *their* heads. Simultaneously we seemed to be enveloped in a cloud. The air felt thick to breathe, although it wasn't damp. My whole body tingled. I had never experienced anything like it. Perhaps even more astonishing, we definitely heard Galilean fishermen speaking Berber, despite the fact that it must actually have been Aramaic. We weren't alone; Jews from all parts of the Diaspora heard them as if they were speaking in their native language. Of course, some in the crowd remained cynical and claimed we were all drunk. In a way we were, but drunk on the Holy Spirit, not on alcohol. (Peter's defence, that it was only three hours after sunrise, was not a knock-out argument to some!) The words of the prophet Joel, which he quoted, and his insistence that the 'last days' to which these referred had been instigated by the arrival, death and resurrection of Yeshua cut many of us to the heart.

And it shall come to pass in the last days, saith the Lord, I will pour out my Spirit upon all flesh: and your sons and your daughters shall prophesy, and your young men shall see visions, and your old men shall dream dreams: And on my servants and on my handmaidens I will pour out in those days my Spirit; and they shall prophesy: And I will show wonders in heaven above, and signs in the earth beneath; blood, and fire, and vapour of smoke: The sun shall be turned into darkness, and the moon into blood, before that great and notable day of the Lord come: And it shall come to pass, that whosoever shall call on the name of the Lord shall be saved.

We travelled home with several of our neighbours, but already those of us from Cyrene were splitting up. Our group, who had seen the risen Yeshua and believed him to be the Messiah, and another, comprising those who either had seen him, but thought he was a ghost, causing mass hysteria, and those with whom he had had no contact. We tried to explain these momentous events to the non-believers, but to no avail. We walked on air. As our ship approached the port of Alexandria it was dusk and its lighthouse shone out like a beacon of hope in the darkness.

Returning home I reopened our bakery but found it hard to settle. Our lives had been turned upside down. Those of my neighbours who believed began to meet regularly in our home on Thursday evenings, in order to praise the Lord, read the scriptures and pray. We would often experience the tingling sensation and have a strong sense that Yeshua was with us, although we could not see him. It was as if he was the yeast and we were the dough, being infused, lifted, and raised by him. The events were so momentous I couldn't stop myself talking about them to everyone who entered our shop.

Fairly soon we began to get opposition. The leaders of the synagogue summoned me and told me to stop talking about the events in Jerusalem and my belief that Yeshua was the Messiah. I said that I could not do so as I knew it to be true. So they threw me and my sons out of the synagogue, as they did the others who so believed. In some ways that was social death, as our neighbours and former friends stopped associating with us. The boys were no longer welcome in their houses and would certainly not be marrying their daughters. Then the synagogue organised a boycott of my bakery and put pressure on our miller not to supply us with flour. I almost went bankrupt. However, the Lord is faithful. At that moment Janni Bar-Joseph sailed into Cyrene and came to dine. I explained what was happening and he arranged for a flour supply to be sent from an Alexandrian miller who was also in the Way. He used the finest Egyptian wheat and soon customers returned, as we now sold the best bread and pastries in Cyrene.

We were able to offer hospitality to travellers, especially those who followed the Way, and word of the risen Lord spread along the coast. We kept open house, welcoming anyone in need, whatever their beliefs. After a couple of years we were attacked again. Some men, probably incited by synagogue leaders, attempted to burn down the bakery. Our shop front was damaged but those who were sleeping upstairs got out uninjured. The arsonists weren't the smartest; firstly they forgot that bakers work through the small hours of the night, so we were alerted to the fire immediately. Secondly, it is almost impossible to burn down a bread oven!

Belief in the Way has split up families. One, which had been coming to our Thursday meetings, drifted away, all except their daughter, Joanna. Her father wanted her to marry a non-believer. She refused and risked bringing shame on her family with potentially disastrous consequences, especially for her. Happily, Alexander had taken a shine to her and so we welcomed her into our home as his wife. Having lost our Joanna all those years ago, I now have a daughter-in-law who could not be a better daughter to me and has blessed us with my grandchildren, Simeon and Salome.

Years passed as we waited for Yeshua to return in glory. Some doubted and left our community and the rest of us began to get discouraged. Janni was a lifeline, keeping us in touch with believers in Alexandria, Caesarea, Jerusalem and Antioch. Rufus has developed a head for business and now acts as the agent for Heli and Janni here in Cyrene. He negotiates with the buyers and sellers of the goods they trade, and manages their warehouse.

Three years ago, as you may know, the harvest failed and what little grain there was shot up in price. Alexander had taken over the business, because I had been having breathing difficulties, which tend to afflict millers and bakers. We thought we were facing ruin, but it was miraculous. Every time we got down to our last of sack of flour and jar of oil, more appeared in our storeroom. We were the only bakers with bread in town, and so were able to stay in business and feed the destitute.

We have been changed for ever. I have seen the hand of the Father in so many people's lives, such that I have to believe that all things work together for good for those who love the Lord, who are called according to His purpose. He has given us grace upon grace and truly offered us a life worth living.

With Alexander, Joanna and Rufus, I, Simon, send to you our warmest greetings and may the blessing of the Lord Almighty, Father, Son and Holy Spirit be with you always.

John 1:1-18

In the beginning was the Word, and the Word was with God, and the Word was God.
The same was in the beginning with God.
All things were made by him; and without him was not any thing made that was made.
In him was life; and the life was the light of men.
And the light shineth in darkness; and the darkness comprehended it not.
There was a man sent from God, whose name was John.
The same came for a witness, to bear witness of the light, that all men through him might believe.
He was not that light, but was sent to bear witness of that light.
That was the true light, which lighteth every man that cometh into the world.
He was in the world, and the world was made by him, and the world knew him not.
He came unto his own, and his own received him not. But as many as received him, to them gave he power to become the sons of God, even to them that believe on his name:
Which were born, not of blood, nor of the will of the flesh, nor of the will of man, but of God. And the Word was made flesh, and dwelt among us (and we beheld his glory, the glory as of the only begotten of the Father),
full of grace and truth.
John bare witness of him, and cried, saying, This was he of whom I spake, He that cometh after me is preferred before me: for he was before me.

And of his fullness have all we received, and grace for grace.
For the law was given by Moses, but grace and truth came
by Jesus Christ.
No man hath seen God at any time; the only begotten Son,
which is in the bosom of the Father, he hath declared him.

GLOSSARY

bar mitzvah: According to Jewish law, when Jewish boys become 13, they become accountable for their actions and become a bar mitzvah, meaning 'one who is subject to the law'. Consequently, they are treated more as adults than as children.

Decapolis: A group of ten cities on the eastern edge of the Roman Empire, i.e. in Judea and Syria. Their culture was Graeco-Roman rather than Jewish.

disciples: The followers of Jesus/Yeshua. He chose twelve men to be his closest companions, representing the twelve tribes of Israel. However, during his ministry various named women, such as his mother, Magda (Mary Magdalene), and others also accompanied him on his travels and supported him financially.

falafel: Deep-fried balls of ground-up chickpeas.

Gentile: A non-Jew.

Last Supper: Jesus' final meal with his disciples held in an upper room in Jerusalem at Passover time. The synoptic gospels (Matthew, Mark and Luke) describe Jesus instigating the sharing of bread and wine as a memorial of him, his life, death and message. John's Gospel describes how he washed his disciples' feet, as a metaphor, inaugurating their future lives of mutual service.

Law: Initially the Ten Commandments found in Exodus 20. Later, the many supplementary commands and prohibitions found in Leviticus, and in other parts of the Hebrew Scriptures.

Magus: A member of an ancient Persian priestly caste, plural Magi. They were skilled in magic and astronomy. The Magi refers to the 'wise men' from the East in Matthew's Gospel account of the birth of Jesus.

money-changer: The Temple only accepted Temple currency, so to give offerings it was necessary to change Roman and other currencies into Temple coinage. They had a reputation for charging unfavourable exchange rates.

Pharisee: A member of the lay rather than priestly group who were experts in the law and who brokered power between the Jewish aristocracy and the masses. Pharisees specialised in issues of ritual purity and tithing (giving ten per cent of your income to the Temple), and believed in the afterlife, judgement, and a densely populated, organised spirit world.

Phylactery: A small leather box containing four texts of scripture written in Hebrew, historically worn by Jews during morning prayer on every day except the Sabbath as a reminder of the obligation to keep the Law. Large ones were worn to imply zealous piety.

priest: The priestly cast came from the tribe of Levi and had no tribal land of their own but were dedicated to serving in the Temple in Jerusalem, their material needs being supplied by all the other tribes of Israel.

Promised Land: The land promised by God to Abraham as a

homeland for the Jewish people. Its borders were defined as being from the east bank of the river Nile in the south, up to the river Euphrates in the north, with the Mediterranean to the west.

Psalm: A song of praise, worship and/or lament, of which there are 150 in the Hebrew Scriptures (The Old Testament). Many are attributed to King David, who lived around 1000 BC.

rabbi: a religious teacher.

Sadducee: Member of a Jewish group who were influential with the aristocracy, who only considered the first five books of the Bible, the **Torah,** to have divine authority and who did not believe in life after death.

Sanhedrin: The supreme Jewish religious, political and legal council in Jerusalem.

Temple: The first Temple in Jerusalem was built by King Solomon, son of King David. It was where God was deemed to reside in the Holy of Holies, a small room containing the Ark of the Covenant. It was destroyed in 587 BC by the Babylonian king Nebuchadnezzar. The Temple building of Jesus' time was constructed by Herod the Great. It was a large complex, with an outer courtyard to which everyone had access and then inner spaces only accessible to Jews.

Torah: The first five books of the Hebrew Scriptures, (The Old Testament), viz. Genesis, Exodus, Leviticus, Numbers and Deuteronomy.

AUTHOR'S NOTE

The structure of this story is based around the three days Jesus went missing in Jerusalem when he was a twelve-year-old boy, as described in Luke's Gospel, and the period between Good Friday and Easter Sunday, using a mixture of Gospel accounts. I have adhered to scripture in the details we have, and allowed my imagination to fill in what might have happened to the protagonists during the gaps in the narrative. Most of the persons mentioned are biblically attested. I have assumed some extra relations in Jesus' family and given him siblings, even though Orthodox and Roman Catholic traditions have it that Mary remained a virgin after Jesus' birth. The Aramaic has no word for 'cousin', and that which is translated as 'brethren' in the King James Authorised Version may refer to all the related children of one generation. However, I have assumed that James, who became the head of the Jerusalem Church, and who is described as one of Jesus' brethren, was in fact a younger brother. This decision is not material to the story as I have told it.

I have used the King James Authorised Version for biblical quotes, except where they are passed off as current speech, to parallel the fact that in the first century AD the scriptures would have been known in either Hebrew or the Greek translation known as the *Septuagint*. Both of these would have been somewhat archaic to the speakers.

I have used the Aramaic version of Jesus - i.e. 'Yeshua', to distance the story slightly from the Gospels for those who would find it difficult to read words put into Jesus' mouth and for non-believers, who might just like to read the tale. I have

147

also named *Philetus*, meaning *beloved*, the 'disciple whom Jesus loved' as spoken of in John's Gospel. This is to avoid taking a stand on whether he was John the Evangelist, the writer of the Gospel and/or whether that John was one of Zebedee's sons. Neither issue is relevant to this story.

According to Josephus, Herod the Great died in 4 BC. Consequently, I have assumed Jesus was born in c. 7 BC. The ages of the historical figures have been estimated on this basis, given the dates we have for them. For example, Annas was High Priest between AD 6 and 15, being dismissed when he was thirty-six. His son-in-law, Caiaphas, was appointed High Priest in AD 18 and was removed from office shortly after Pilate's dismissal in late 36 or early 37. Consequently, I have assumed he was not that much younger than his father-in-law, so when Jesus was twelve Caiaphas would have been around twenty to twenty-five years old.

I have used Richard Bauckham's suggestion in *Jesus and the Eyewitnesses* (Wm. B Eerdmans Publishing, USA, 2006), that the young man who runs away naked in Gethsemane, as attested by Mark's Gospel, was Lazarus, whom Jesus had raised from the dead. His father I have named Eleazar, which in Hebrew means 'God is my help,' as does Lazarus.

I have described Simon of Cyrene as a red-head, despite the fact that he is sometimes portrayed as a sub-Saharan African. He named his sons Rufus (implying red hair, which might have run in the family), and Alexander, indicating a cosmopolitan outlook for a North African Jew. Cyrenaica is the eastern part of Libya and most locals look Mediterranean. In fact, during the overthrow of Colonel Gaddafi, his foreign mercenaries were primarily identified by being sub-Saharan Africans.

I have described post-resurrection images on Yeshua's shroud as being similar to those on the Shroud of Turin. That is made of linen, the style of weaving of which has been identified as being consistent with that from the first-century Near East. It has traces of limestone dust on it, local pollen and the image of the front and back of a man showing all the marks of Christ's Passion. How the image was formed remains a mystery, as no pigment has been detected and the bloodstains appear to have been applied before the image - unlikely in a fake. The image resembles a faint photographic negative with the body as the light source. Carbon dating, which was performed in the 1980s, suggested a fourteenth-century origin. However, small pieces from the edge of the fabric were used, which appear to have been from those sections repaired by Poor Clare nuns in the sixteenth century, following damage in a fire. This would confuse the results. More information may be obtained from Ian Wilson's *The Shroud: The 2000-year-old Mystery Solved* (Bantam Press 2010).

Suggested further reading, in suggested reading order.

The New Testament, preferably a modern English version, for example, the New Revised Standard Version or the New International Version.

Questions of Life: An opportunity to explore the meaning of life, Nicky Gumbel, (Kingsway Publications, Eastbourne, UK, 1993). A text of the **Alpha Course**, www.alpha.org.uk, an introduction to Christianity.

Jesus: A Very Short Introduction, Richard Bauckham, (Oxford University Press, UK, 2011).

The Gospels and Jesus, Graham N. Stanton, (Oxford University Press, UK 1989).

Jesus and the Eyewitnesses, Richard Bauckham, (Wm. B Eerdmans Publishing, Grand Rapids, Michigan, USA, 2006).

The Shroud: The 2000-year-old Mystery Solved, Ian Wilson, (Bantam Press, UK,2010).

The Resurrection of the Son of God, N.T. Wright, (SPCK, London, 2003)

Dictionary of New Testament Background, (Eds. Craig A Evans & Stanley E Porter, IVP USA 2000).

Author photo: Jet Photographic

THE AUTHOR

The Reverend Sonia Falaschi-Ray is a priest in the Church of England, ministering in and around Cambridge. For much of her adult life she was an agnostic, coming to a living faith on an Alpha Course at Holy Trinity Brompton in 1998. Having had careers in engineering and finance, she graduated in Theology and Religious Studies from the University of Cambridge and studied for the ministry at Ridley Hall, an Anglican theological training college. She lives in Hertfordshire with her husband John and golden retrievers Quintus and Rufus.

Her previous book, *Harry Potter: a Christian Chronicle*, published by The Book Guild, Brighton, 2011, examines the parallels between characters in J. K. Rowling's novels and those in the Bible, as well as the moral framework, Christian symbolism, world view and ethic of the series.